"I want you, Brianna!"

His hands swept down her back and bracketed her hips. He kissed her again and again. Without any conscious thought at all, Brianna moved with him—and against him—in an erotic rhythm that slowly dissolved all coherent thought.

Wanting his skin against hers, she worked fiercely at the buttons of her cashmere dress, and as they gave way his mouth broke from hers to explore. Every touch of his questing lips on her skin tightened the coil of hunger inside her.

She gasped and dug her fingers into his biceps as he brought her naked breasts to an aching hardness. A groan welled up in her throat. "Love me now, Evan!" she demanded.

An odd, sudden stillness arrested his movements—as if some alien force had stunned him.

"Evan?" she whispered against his shoulder, alarmed at his reaction. She struggled to see his face, but when she tried to move, his arms tightened with brutal strength, holding her fast.

In a whisper softer than a kiss, he asked, "*What* did you call me?"

"Call you?" she asked, bewildered. "Why, nothing. All I said was…" She stopped, his name poised on her lips. All she had called him was Evan. The full force of her bizarre realization hit her in a blinding rush and she pulled away in horror. "You're not *Evan!*"

His dark blue gaze bored mercilessly into her. "'Fraid not."

Dear Reader,

The idea of identical twins has always fascinated me. I've known pairs who look so much alike they could easily pass for each other. Imagine the complications that might arise...either by error or design...especially when one twin ends up in the wrong bed!

Those complications would deepen if a woman fancied herself in love with one twin and positively despised the other. If that "bad boy" twin happened to be a wickedly charming rogue who has always delighted in tormenting this particular woman—for reasons he alone knows— we have a recipe for emotional dynamite.

In this story our heroine sets off just the right spark to ignite that dynamite. Hope you enjoy the fireworks!

All the best,

Donna Sterling

Books by Donna Sterling

HARLEQUIN TEMPTATION
586—SOMETHING OLD, SOMETHING NEW
628—POSSESSING ELISSA

HIS DOUBLE,
HER TROUBLE
Donna Sterling

Harlequin Books

TORONTO • NEW YORK • LONDON
AMSTERDAM • PARIS • SYDNEY • HAMBURG
STOCKHOLM • ATHENS • TOKYO • MILAN
MADRID • WARSAW • BUDAPEST • AUCKLAND

To my mother-in-law, Leone, who not only raised the perfect husband for me, but also taught me how to watch football, play poker, fish and cook Southern style. I'll always miss you. Also, many thanks to Melissa Beck, Anne Bushyhead, Sandra Chastain, Gin Ellis, Marge Gargosh, Susan Goggins, Carina Rock, Pat Van Wie and Ann White.

ISBN 0-373-25755-4

HIS DOUBLE, HER TROUBLE

Copyright © 1997 by Donna Fejes.

Printed in U.S.A.

1

"YOU HAVEN'T SLEPT WITH him yet? Are you kidding? You've been dating him for six months!"

Ignoring her friend's incredulous stare, Brianna Devon leaned forward on her bedroom vanity stool and carefully finished applying a second coat of mascara—one coat more than she'd ever worn before. "Are you sure this much mascara won't look...you know... cheap?" Doubtfully she studied the effect in the mirror.

Chloe rolled her eyes and shook her auburn locks, which had been expensively styled to look disheveled. "Go ahead, Bri, get wild and crazy. *Dare* to wear two coats of mascara." With an affectionate smirk, Chloe rested a hand on a slender hip, her French-tipped nails gleaming. "Would I tell you to do *anything* that might result in 'cheap'?"

Brianna slanted her an apologetic grin. She'd forgotten whom she was talking to—the town's resident queen of chic. She'd called in the "big guns" to prepare for tonight.

"So what's the problem?" persisted Chloe as she raked Brianna's tawny waves into an artful disarray that cascaded to her shoulders—shoulders left brazenly bare by her new sweater dress. "Why haven't you gone to bed with him yet? You've been friends since high school, so it's not like you don't know him well enough. Just last month you were telling me how your friendship has 'blossomed into love.' You're not kids anymore; you're pushing thirty. So what's stopping you?" With a sudden thought, Chloe narrowed her eyes in the mirror. "He *does* want to, doesn't he?"

"Very much," Brianna replied, unwilling to raise doubts about Evan's virility. After a moment, though, she admitted, "At least, he *did* want to. But I...well, I haven't allowed our relationship to go much beyond the kissing stage."

"Kissing stage?" The concept was evidently foreign to Chloe. "What have you been doing, slapping his hands away?"

Brianna winced. "Not slapping. More like...evading." In quiet misery, she added, "The last time we were together, he didn't even kiss me. It's like he's given up. He thinks he doesn't turn me on."

"Gee, whatever gave him *that* impression?"

"I'm going through with it tonight, though," she vowed, "come hell or high water."

"What hell, what high water?" Chloe cried, lifting her hands in bewilderment. "It couldn't be your first time, could it? You dated that pre-med student back in college for your entire freshman year, and plenty of guys since then."

"No, it wouldn't be my first time, but I feel that when it comes to sex, it's better to err on the side of caution."

"How cautious can you get? You told me that since Evan moved back here, you and he have fallen in love. Have you changed your mind?"

"Absolutely not. Our relationship transcends the physical. We have a true communion of the mind, of the spirit. He's intelligent, sincere, dependable, ambitious— everything I want in a man."

And he'll never own me. Although Brianna didn't voice the words, she knew this was the most important aspect of any relationship she'd ever have. Her mate would have to respect her need for self-reliance. She'd earn her own money, build her own credit, maintain her own house that no one could make her leave. Her career would be her top priority. No relationship of hers would ever turn into an economic prison....

And yet, she wanted a loving relationship. At times, she yearned for it. How many men in the world would understand her as Evan did?

"You'd be nuts to let him get away," pronounced Chloe.

Brianna bit her lip. "It might be too late. He hasn't called me in two weeks. Of course, he *has* been out of the country on business." But she knew that business had never kept him from calling before. Was she losing him? Losing her chance to find out if he truly *was* the man she loved?

With a renewed sense of mission, she turned back to the mirror and smoothed on sultry, gleaming lipstick—shades deeper than her usual gloss. She'd put an end to their estrangement tonight. She'd compensate him for the frustration she'd caused him; make it well worth his wait.

"If you don't want him, I know plenty of women who do," warned Chloe. "He's a Harvard grad, rich, and CEO of the biggest firm in town—the firm *you work for*, I might add."

"That has nothing to do with my feelings for him!" In fact, she wished Evan *wasn't* her boss. She hated to think that her position as human resources director might be attributed to their relationship. She'd earned a degree and worked nine long years to achieve that title. Evan had lived away in Boston for most of that time. He'd come back home only three years ago to take over as CEO.

When he'd first come back to Pleasantville, they'd met as old friends, happy to see each other and reminisce about high school. Conscious of their co-workers, though, Brianna had discouraged his attentions to avoid the appearance of favoritism. It hadn't been easy; Evan had been determined to renew their friendship, to deepen it into something more.

And she'd thoroughly enjoyed his company. She had, after all, nursed a secret crush on him in high school, although he'd been dating someone far prettier than she at the time. And he *had* grown into the living embodiment of her ideal man. It seemed foolish to continue turning down dates with him just because they worked for the same firm. Yet she couldn't help feeling sensitive about dating her boss.

"I know your relationship with Evan doesn't have squat to do with your career," Chloe assured her. "I just meant he's a real catch. And to top it off, he's a genuine Adonis. Most women would give anything to be in Evan Rowland's bed." Chloe's mouth curled in a smile. "Although personally, I'd prefer Jake's. I have a soft spot for bad boys."

At the mention of Evan's twin brother, Brianna dropped her lipstick into her purse and clicked it shut with a resounding *snap*. "There's no accounting for taste."

Chloe let out a brief laugh. "Oh, I forgot. Jake's been a thorn in your side since high school, hasn't he? But you've got to admit, he's an attractive thorn."

"Physically attractive, yes. He *is* identical to Evan. But only in appearance. That's where the similarity ends."

"They both inherited their parents' fortune," Chloe pointed out, "which means they're both filthy rich."

"Which isn't necessarily a plus." With money came power—and power could be used to hurt as well as to help. Her mother had married a man with considerable income and had entrusted her future to him. Look where it had gotten her. Trapped—under his thumb—for too many painful years, then unable to support herself when the marriage had ended.

Brianna wrenched her thoughts away from hurtful topics. "No amount of money could ever make up for Jake's lack of moral character. He's an irresponsible, womanizing troublemaker." Just the thought of him raised her blood pressure—and brought to mind his wicked blue-eyed gaze, which made her stomach clench in a disturbing way. "He has a new bimbo on his arm every time he comes to town."

"Yeah, and they all have expensive jewelry and good tans. I wouldn't mind jet-setting with him for a while."

Thoroughly annoyed, Brianna turned away from Chloe and fastened pearls to her earlobes. She didn't want to think about Jake Rowland tonight. She wanted to forget his very existence. Because even though she'd never admit it, he was at the root of her problem. When Evan became aroused and gazed at her with that certain gleam in his eyes, his dark brown hair all tousled and glowing golden, his intent clearly sexual, he reminded her too much of Jake!

Jake had always been the one who undressed her with his eyes—Brianna and every other reasonably attractive female he came across. The hell of it was, once she started thinking about Jake and all the rotten stunts he'd pulled on her, the humiliation he'd always caused her, the dread she'd carried around in her heart at the very possibility of running into him, her sensuous mood with Evan was blown.

Rising from the vanity stool, Brianna gazed critically at her transformed self in the wall mirror. The black, off-the-shoulder cashmere dress she'd bought for the occasion molded sleekly to her body—a far cry from her usual discreet suits or slacks. "How do I look?"

"Stunning," pronounced Chloe.

"From the moment I walk in his door, I want him to know that tonight's special." And though it was true, she also knew that the makeover was as much for her own benefit as for his. She needed to immerse herself in sensuality to get into the mood, to *stay* in the mood. To carry her past mental distractions. "I want him to be so consumed with passion that he sweeps me away to another dimension."

"So he doesn't sweep you away, huh?"

"I didn't mean it like that." In all fairness, she couldn't blame her lack of passion on Evan. He couldn't help having a reprobate brother who looked exactly like him. "Thanks for helping with my femme fatale makeover, Chloe. My confidence is at an all-time high."

"If you change your mind and back out again, let me know," Chloe ordered as Brianna walked her to the front door. "I'll make you an appointment with a sex therapist."

Mildly alarmed at the prospect, Brianna assured her that a therapist wouldn't be necessary. Looking doubtful, Chloe left for her own Friday night date.

Brianna returned to her bedroom, spritzed on provocative cologne and glanced one last time in the mirror. She barely recognized herself. Wouldn't Evan be surprised at the change? Her appearance alone should make it perfectly clear that she was ready for him tonight. She'd let nothing get in their way this time...especially not thoughts of Jake.

At least she didn't have to worry about him showing up in person. He'd been jet-setting around the globe for years now. The few times he'd been back for brief visits had been bad enough.

At a charity fund-raiser while she'd been dancing with Evan—a rare treat, since they hadn't been dating yet—Jake had cut in, *insisted* she dance with him, then waltzed them both into the swimming pool. He claimed to have lost his footing. Brianna knew he'd done it on purpose.

During another visit, he'd sent her a singing telegram for her birthday—in the middle of her speech at the civic club. A man in a cop uniform stormed in, handcuffed her to the microphone, then proceeded to sing, prance and shed his clothes all around her. Jake must have paid him generously—*nothing* had stopped the young man from stripping down to that ridiculous loincloth and gyrating beside her. At the back of the room had stood Jake Rowland, with amusement brimming in his eyes. Brianna's fists tightened at the memory.

She was glad, more than glad, that he rarely visited their small hometown. But she wouldn't think about Jake tonight. No matter what.

Shrugging into her soft black coat, she strode out of her bungalow and into the crisp October air, her high heels clicking against the stone front steps. Evan would be home from his business trip by now. His flight had been due to arrive this afternoon.

She'd give him a pleasant welcome home after his two weeks away. A very pleasant welcome home. By the time she was finished with him, Evan would have no doubts left about her capability of enjoying hot, steamy sex with him.

Hopefully *she'd* have no doubts left, either.

EVAN'S TOWNHOUSE, which was actually owned by his family, along with the entire downtown area and the five-story office building behind it, looked welcoming with a flickering glow in its windows that told of a fire in the hearth.

At least she knew he was home. With a shiver of nervousness, she hesitated on the doorstep. What if he wasn't alone?

After less than a minute, she shook her head at her own anxiety. Evan wouldn't have another woman at his apartment without breaking off their relationship first. He prided himself on his decency and fairness in all matters. It was one of the things she loved so much about him.

Extending a hand that slightly trembled, she rang the bell. When there was no response, she breathed a sigh of relief. Acute relief. She realized then that if he *had* opened the door, she might not have gone through with it. How disastrous that would have been! He'd have thought her the worst kind of tease—dressed for seduction, dropping by for an unexpected evening visit…then refusing to make love. Perhaps it was for the best that he hadn't answered.

Just as she turned to go, the door swung open.

Evan peered out at her, his hair damp as if it had been towel dried, his broad chest and muscled shoulders bare. He wore only a bath towel fastened at his lean waist. He stared at her in blank surprise.

Brianna stared back at him, speechless. She hadn't expected him to answer the door half-naked. She'd seen him shirtless before, of course, and in swimming trunks that had covered even less than his towel did now. But the sun-bronzed masculine splendor of his form and face evoked a deep feminine appreciation that hadn't hit her with such force in quite some time. He was simply the most breathtaking man she'd ever seen.

"Brianna!" Pleasant surprise sounded in his deep-timbered voice. She'd never before paid him a visit without calling in advance. He leaned against the doorjamb and a lazy smile lifted one side of his mouth, deepening a vertical crease alongside it. "Long time no see."

Held motionless by that smile, Brianna felt a sensual pooling of warmth deep within her. And suddenly the idea of seduction didn't seem so cumbersome. In fact, it took on a definite allure. Maybe she was ready, after all.

"It *has* been long," she murmured. "Too long." Brushing past him on her way into the apartment, she removed her coat and turned her face up to his, inexplicably breathless as her gaze played over his handsome features. Perhaps it was her own frame of mind, but something about his answering stare packed a more powerful punch than she'd expected. Shivery anticipation swept through her. And they hadn't even touched yet!

Emboldened by the good beginning, she tossed her coat onto a chair and kissed him lightly on the lips. Desire curled through her.

When she drew back, the surprise—which hadn't left his gaze—had intensified, and she remembered the changes in her own appearance: her hair, her makeup, her sexy sweater dress, her high spiked heels...quite a difference from her usual understated style. She'd never been a femme fatale before. She rather enjoyed the effect it was obviously having on him. He looked nothing short of thunderstruck.

"Thought I'd welcome you home," she purred.

He continued to stare, his gaze leaving her face to slowly absorb the rest of her. She began to feel flustered. She wasn't used to this role of aggressor. When his eyes returned to hers, a new, tangible tension charged the air, and she wished he'd take over from here. Surely he'd guessed her intentions! But he made no move toward her at all. In fact, he hadn't even shut the door.

She wet her lips, which had somehow gone dry. "I...I thought I'd surprise you."

"Oh, you did that."

Second thoughts about her impulsive visit and the purpose behind it fluttered in her stomach like butterflies. "You...you don't have plans for tonight, do you?"

"None that can't include you." His soft drawled reply did strange things to her pulse as he shut the door and locked it. "Make yourself at home." He gestured toward the sofa in front of the fireplace, where a small but robust fire crackled. "Guess I'll go throw some clothes on."

Afraid of losing her sensuous mood with too much time to think, she reached out and touched his arm. The muscles of his biceps tightened reflexively beneath her fingers. He felt harder tonight, sexier—and her mood deepened into a physical longing. "No, don't," she implored. "You'd only have to take them off again."

His dark brows drew together, and his stare could only be called stunned. "Why exactly are you here, Brianna?" he asked, his voice hushed and his gaze intent.

So he wasn't going to make this easy for her. Self-consciously she withdrew her hand from his arm. But she did manage to whisper with a pretense of boldness, "I'm ready. I've come here to...you know..."

"No, I'm not sure that I do."

She felt her cheeks grow warm. He evidently didn't want to deal with her rejection again...or else he no longer wanted her. "I'm ready to make love to you." In spite of herself, she added on a whisper, "If you want to."

Something flared within his midnight blue eyes, something deep and smoky and powerful. "Mind if I ask what brought about this change? I mean, I can't think of a better welcome home, but—"

"I've had a lot of time to think while you were gone, and I...well, I realized that I've loved you too long to lose this chance." Building up her courage to touch him again, she laid her palm against his freshly shaven face, then caressed her way to his strong square jaw. "Did you know that even back in high school, I wanted to be more than just friends?"

"With me?"

"Yes, with you!" The incredulity of his response—the fact that he hadn't known and that he found it so surprising—endeared him even more to her. He hadn't been ignoring her desire to deepen their friendship into a romance; he'd simply been unaware of it. "I don't have much experience at this seduction thing," she whispered, slipping her arms around his neck and gazing at him in earnest appeal, "so whenever you're ready, feel free to jump right in."

"Brianna," he breathed, his gaze dancing with hers in a slow, sultry tango as she wove her fingers into the thick, damp locks at the nape of his neck, "are you sure?"

"I've never been more sure." And she realized it was

true. Never had she wanted him more. As lines furrowed between his brows and a question formed on his lips, she laid her finger prohibitively against them. "Shh. No more talk. Let's just do it."

His gaze underwent a subtle change—a kind of wonder replaced the questions. His strong, warm arms came up around her and he kissed the fingertip she'd laid against his lips...then drew it in with a sucking motion that sent erotic sensations sizzling to every private part of her. She withdrew her finger in weak-kneed surprise. He'd never done anything like that before.

Still holding her gaze, he met her in a tentative tasting kiss. Brianna closed her eyes and savored it. He tasted smooth as brandy, potent as rum. Before she had a chance to reflect anymore on this unexpected delight, the kiss moved and flowed to a new intensity.

The scents of soap and something stirringly male emanated from his skin and hair with the growing warmth. A need like she'd never known kindled deep inside her.

The parries and thrusts of their tongues gradually turned from graceful to demanding. His strong fingers plunged into her hair and held her fast against him as he slanted his mouth this way and that to draw the most from every kiss. He nipped at her bottom lip, drew it into his mouth and slowly released it. She thought she'd swoon from the pleasure.

Hoarsely he whispered, "I do want you, Brianna!" His hands swept down her back and bracketed her hips to his. He kissed her again and again. Without any conscious thought at all, she moved with him—and against him—in an erotic rhythm that slowly dissolved all coherent thought.

The soft cashmere of her dress had to go. She wanted his skin against hers. Her fingers worked fiercely at the buttons, and as they gave way his mouth broke from hers to explore. Every touch of his questing mouth on her skin tightened the coil of hunger inside her.

He tugged the dress partway down. She pushed it the rest of the way. Deftly he unhooked her strapless bra and tossed it aside, freeing her breasts. A groan tore from his throat as he captured them in his hands. His tongue edged around one highly sensitive bud...and then flicked lightly across it.

She gasped, dug her fingers into his biceps and pressed against him. He suckled her to an aching hardness.

Liquid fire pumped through her. He swept her up into his arms, his eyes burning sexual messages into hers as he carried her away from the flickering firelight, through cool shadows in the corridor, to a bedroom where he laid her down. Without breaking contact, he joined her, mouth to mouth, body to body.

She reveled in the taste, the textures of his mouth, his skin, his hair, as she slipped deeper into a world of pure sensation, pure desire. She was movement and heat, friction and rhythm, blinding flashes and velvet darkness.

Openmouthed kisses glanced off her neck, her breasts, her abdomen. Heat throbbed everywhere he moved; aching need built everywhere he didn't. He swept his tongue in a lingering path just above her bikini lace. A groan welled up in her throat. She *wanted*. Frantically wanted...

Soft, mewling cries escaped her as he dipped within her panties, kissing and licking, working his way down. Driving her into a swelter.

And then he touched her, the very core of her, with one warm, moist glide of his tongue. It was more than she could stand. Quicksilver pleasure pitched her right over the edge.

With a shuddering cry, she doubled over. Waves of reaction hit her, deep crimson flashed before her eyes and she found herself quaking helplessly, enfolded in his embrace. "I d-didn't know," she finally gasped. "I didn't know it could b-be like this."

He tightened his arms around her, and his heartbeat thundered against her ear. "I didn't, either." She felt the heat in him, like a fever, and the iron-strong tension still coiled in every muscle of his body.

When she was better able to speak, she said in a concerned rush, "But *you*...you haven't..."

"Don't worry," he said with a tight, breathless laugh, "I will." He reached down between their bodies and tugged at something wrapped around her knees. Her panties, she realized. "Have to take these off," he whispered, trying his best to do so without releasing his hold on her. With a few smooth moves, she slid the wispy lace down her legs and out of their way.

With a slow animal grace, his muscles shifted until his lithe body covered hers, pinning her beneath. She arched provocatively against him, the heat flaring again within her. "Right now, Brianna," he breathed in an urgent whisper. "Let's go there now."

She wrapped her arms around him and commandeered his mouth in a thorough kiss. His hardness swelled against her inner thighs. The muscles in his back bunched and flexed beneath her palms as he undulated with tightly controlled grace, dominating their motion, his hardness probing against her softness.

"Yes, now," she groaned, feverish with renewed wanting. "Love me now, Evan!"

An odd, sudden stillness arrested his movement—as if some alien force had literally stunned him.

"Evan?" she whispered against his shoulder, alarmed at the way he had stiffened into absolute immobility. "What's wrong?" Thoughts about strokes and aneurysms and all kinds of horrible conditions raced through her mind. She struggled to see his face, but he had turned his head and his silky dark hair blinded her. When she tried to move, his arms tightened with brutal strength, holding her fast in place. "For heaven's sake, *what's wrong?*" she gasped, squeezed nearly breathless.

She heard his pent-up breath rush out as if forced between clenched teeth. Then he buried his face in the curve of her neck.

"Evan?" she tried again in a tiny whisper, frightened and concerned.

"Don't...say...anything," he ground out between teeth that were obviously still clenched. She felt a light but discernible tremor pass through him. Then another.

After an anxious moment, she ventured, "Are you okay?"

"No."

She pressed her jaw against his temple and waited. For what, she wasn't sure.

When he finally made a move, it was one she hadn't expected—he levered himself up on his forearms until his body barely touched hers, and he stared down at her with a fine sheen of sweat on his flushed rugged face and a smoldering intensity in his eyes. In a whisper softer than a kiss, he asked, "What did you call me?"

"Call you?" she said, entirely bewildered. "Why, nothing. All I said was..." She stopped, his name poised on her lips. All she'd called him was *Evan.*

It was then that the first inkling of disaster spiraled

through her. Not a full-blown realization—just a bizarre supposition, too terrible to entertain.

His dark blue gaze bore mercilessly into her. His eyebrows rose, and he prompted, "All you said was...?"

She then noticed his hair. It had dried considerably since he'd first ushered her into his apartment. It waved in thick, unruly locks around his sun-bronzed face. In a trance, she reached up and touched the dark brown hair that glinted liberally with gold. It was a good inch longer than it had been when he'd left town...two short weeks ago.

She gaped at that hair in mute disbelief. Her stare shifted to his face. A familiar beloved face. But when she examined him closer, she found the telltale scar—a tiny white line almost hidden by the sweep of his dark winged brows. A high-school football injury, she remembered.

But Evan hadn't been the one to play football. He'd been president of the student council, editor of the yearbook and champion of the chess club—not some arrogant, swaggering quarterback *with a scar underneath his left eyebrow.*

His wide, firm mouth tightened, and with one fluid motion he rolled clear of her, onto his side. Propping himself up on one arm, he faced her, wordlessly watching as she lay there grappling with the dawning truth.

The full force of it hit her in a blinding rush, and in a whisper bleak with horror she gasped, "You're not Evan!"

His expression didn't change, but his gaze remained steadfast. "'Fraid not."

2

IF THE EARTH had fallen off its axis, if the sun had ceased to burn, she couldn't have felt any deeper horror. Her reality shattered and she desperately strained to fit the fragments back together, to make sense of the absurd.

He *had* to be Evan. *Had* to be...

"Evan is still in France," came the deep, quiet, disembodied voice from somewhere beside her.

But Evan had answered the door when she'd arrived, hadn't he? She'd kissed him hello, told him that she wanted to make love. "Oh, God," Brianna whispered, her eyes wide and unseeing as she pressed her hand to her mouth.

Then there were the kisses—the long, hot kisses that she had initiated. "Oh, God." She squeezed her eyes shut to block them out, but the memory reeled forward.

She'd unbuttoned her dress. He'd kissed her everywhere, in the most intimate of ways. And he'd brought her to the most shattering climax of her entire life. He'd held her quivering in his arms...and begging for more....

"Oh, God!" she cried in painful mortification. Rolling over onto a bed pillow, she buried her face in her arms. Jake Rowland! Her nemesis, her enemy.

"Brianna—" The hoarse masculine voice washed over her with an intimacy that now shocked her. This man wasn't Evan! He had no right to say her name in such a low, caressing tone. No right to lie so close to her that she felt his body heat radiating clear through her skin.

"Stay away from me," she cried with a sob. "Just stay away from me, Jake." And though he didn't say another word, she felt his gaze, and a hot little shiver went through her, starting at her nape, working its way down her spine and out into her most private regions.

Most private regions? There weren't any that he hadn't already explored! Just thinking of his "explorations" made her quake all over again, made a dry heat steal over her, while chill bumps sprang up on her arms.

Another realization hit her: she was lying here in bed with him—naked!

With a little shriek, she grabbed at the rumpled bedspread and wrapped it around her in a panic. "My clothes," she cried, sitting up straight and thrashing around with one hand while holding on to her cover with the other. "I need my clothes!"

"Calm down." Jake sat up beside her, completely unconcerned with his own golden, muscled nakedness.

"I have to get out of here," she wailed and launched herself off the bed. Dragging the bedspread with her, she searched the floor for her panties...her black lace panties, which Jake Rowland had helped pull down her legs. Those legs trembled beneath her now so violently that she nearly lost her balance.

"Damn it, Brianna, you're not going anywhere until you settle down and we talk this thing through." He sprang to his feet, then circled the bed, stalking her as if she were some wild animal he intended to corner. "You can't get behind the wheel of a car or even walk across a street until you calm down."

Calm down! Nothing could calm her down. *Nothing.* Evan was in France, and she was here, *naked with his brother!* With one wary eye on Jake's approach, she frantically searched by the side of the bed for her underwear...and what about her dress? Where had they dropped it? In the bedroom? In the living room? She couldn't remember...couldn't think straight....

She then caught sight of black lace. Her panties! In Jake's hand! He was gazing at her with grim concern. Or rather what *looked* like grim concern. But this was Jake Rowland, and she knew from long experience just how concerned he'd be about her. She made a move for her underwear. He evaded her reach. "Breathe, Brianna, deep and slow."

"Give them to me!" she cried in seething outrage.

"Not until you—"

He didn't get out another word before she lunged at him, grabbing for the black lace, determined to rip it from his hand. His arms shot out around her. She elbowed him in the ribs. He wrestled her onto the bed and she fought wildly, lashing out with every ounce of her strength. But he overcame her with little effort and held her from behind, his arms wrapped around her midsection, her arms pinned to her sides, her back lodged solidly against him and her cheek pressed to the linen sheets of his bed.

"How could you deceive me like that?" she railed. "How could even *you* stoop so low?"

"I knew you'd find a way to blame this on me."

"You took your brother's place in bed with me!"

"*You* came on to *me*, remember?"

"You knew I thought you were Evan!"

"How was I supposed to know that?"

"Why would I want to go to bed with *you*?"

"I thought you might have finally come to your senses."

Rage rushed through her, hot and blinding. She struggled to free herself from his hold. "Let go of me!"

"I'll let you go when you calm down."

But her anger only grew hotter, and her muscles strained with fury. The more she wrestled, the more he tightened his hold. He moved one arm up across her chest and wrapped an iron-strong leg over hers to subdue her kicks. The bedspread had dropped away from her when she'd first lunged at him. Her writhing brought her against him in full skin-to-skin contact, muscle against muscle, flesh against flesh. Before long, a heat of a very different kind radiated between them. Every twist and wriggle intensified it.

She knew this heat. He'd stoked it earlier—with his kisses, his hands, his mouth. She couldn't help thinking about what he could do with his body. A bolt of desire shot through her and she closed her eyes, nearly overcome by it. She wanted to move her hips, to press her backside against the virile hardness she felt there.

She forced herself into stillness—absolute, breathless stillness. He, too, moved not a muscle. But the tension enveloped them, thick and dangerously flammable.

"I'm...I'm calm now," she finally breathed, although she wasn't in the least bit calm. She blazed inside with a shamefully physical longing.

"Are you sure?" he said in a hot strangled whisper.

She nodded, not trusting her voice.

"Promise you won't bolt if I let you go?"

"I p-promise."

He hesitated, his breathing ragged. Then he slowly removed his leg from over hers, one arm from above her breasts, his other from around her waist.

She couldn't have bolted if she'd wanted to. The struggle had drained her of rage but left her as hot, weak and disoriented as anyone awakening from a fever. That fever still simmered in her blood.

From her side view she saw Jake stand, toss her panties onto the bed, throw open the closet door and shrug into a maroon silk robe. He tied its sash with brusque, impatient tugs, his face dark and sullen. Without the briefest glance at her, he strode from the room, reappearing in the doorway seconds later to throw the rest of her clothes to her. Then he firmly, wordlessly shut the bedroom door.

A WHILE LATER, Brianna emerged fully dressed from the bedroom—the guest suite, she now realized, not the one *Evan* always occupied. Jake stood beside the gray stone hearth, still clad in the maroon silk robe, which left his muscled calves and a shadowy vee of his broad chest bare. He held a steaming mug in his hand. Another mug sat on the end table beside the sofa, obviously waiting for her. The fragrance of freshly brewed coffee beckoned, but she wanted to be gone from here as quickly as possible.

He glanced up from the fire and pointed to the sofa. "Sit."

She raised a brow, considered taking offense, then decided to postpone her protest. He looked ready to tackle her again at the first wrong move. Not that she was intimidated. She simply didn't want to chance any more physical encounters with Jake Rowland. She still felt overly sensitive from the most recent ones.

With her head held high, she sat in the armchair beside the sofa he had indicated, her legs folding beneath her, her arms crossing in a protective hug. Her cashmere dress clung below her bare shoulders and felt far too revealing, now that she knew the identity of the man watching her. Her hair was a wild tangle, impossible to comb. Her lipstick had been thoroughly kissed away, and she refused to freshen it. She didn't want Jake to think she was primping for him.

But despite her resolution to remain uncaring of his opinion, a self-conscious warmth rose in her cheeks beneath his silent stare. It wouldn't have hurt to have at least *glanced* in the mirror, she supposed.

"So what's going on between Evan and you?" he finally asked, his voice low and nonchalant as he set his coffee on the mantel.

"I don't see how that's any of your business."

"Last time I was in town, you two were just old friends. And business associates. At least, that's how *he* seemed to view it. Since when did things, uh, heat up?"

"You didn't know that Evan and I have been dating?"

"He never mentioned it to me, and I've been with him the past couple days in France."

She pressed her lips together, struggling to conceal the hurt that Evan hadn't told his brother anything about her...*if* Jake could be believed. After a moment, she chided herself. Of course he couldn't be believed! This was the guy who had ruined her junior prom by bragging to her date that he was the father of her baby. And she'd never even had a baby! At the time, she'd never even had sex!

"As you well know, Evan and I have always been close," she said. "Lately we've gotten...closer."

It looked as though Jake would say more, but then he glanced away from her, toward the fire. Incredible, how much he resembled Evan. The firelight caught the same golden highlights in his dark hair, cast the same intriguing shadows across the rugged planes of his face. But his stance seemed more aggressive, his presence more dominating.

She reached for the coffee mug, needing something to distract her from the sight of him.

"You don't really believe I intentionally deceived you tonight, do you?" he asked.

Brianna paused with the cup halfway to her mouth. She wasn't ready to discuss tonight's fiasco. Her emotions were still too raw to confront him now. "I wouldn't put it past you," she retorted. "You've pretended to be Evan before."

He frowned—a study in outraged innocence. "When?"

"In high school, the first time I met you. I called you Evan, and asked if I could ride with you to our ecology club earth march."

"What'd I say?"

She swept a lock of hair from her eyes and tucked it behind her ear. "You asked me if I'd 'put out.'"

A reminiscent glow lightened his eyes. "I remember." Though he didn't actually smile, she knew he wasn't far from it. "I never was sure what your answer was...yes or no?"

Her hands tightened around the mug. "It was a good thing I ran into Evan at the other end of the hall or I would have despised him for embarrassing me like that."

"Good lord, Brianna, we were fifteen, sixteen years old. That was the last time I ever pretended to be Evan."

"Until tonight." She set her coffee cup down to keep from spilling it.

His stare locked with hers, generating an intensity that made her heart beat faster. "I swear to you, I thought you knew who I was."

She wished she could believe him. Otherwise she'd have to hate him more than she ever had, and that wouldn't be healthy. "But why would you think I'd proposition *you?*" she asked, at a genuine loss for understanding. "You know I've always gone to great lengths to avoid you."

"Yeah, I'm aware of that." He crossed his arms in an insolent pose, leaning one broad shoulder against the mantel. "But you said you had a change of heart. That you missed me. That you, ah, secretly wanted me even back in high school."

She felt her face blanch at that memory, and she couldn't put the words together to form an effective reply. "You should have known I meant Evan," she murmured weakly.

"Well, I didn't." He took a step toward her, pinning her back into her chair with his gaze. "Don't forget that *I* was the one who stopped in there," he reminded her, cocking his thumb toward the bedroom. "Why do you think I stopped when I did, Brianna? Do you think it was easy?"

"No," she whispered, trying to avoid thinking back to the incident under discussion...to when his hardness had probed her intimately, and she had urged him, begged him, to take her. "I'm sure it couldn't have been easy."

"That's the understatement of the damn century! If I was out to deceive you, why didn't I go all the way?"

It took her a moment to come up with a likely reason, but when she did, she proclaimed it with passion. "Because you knew that if you had, Evan or I would have killed you."

He gaped at her in amazement. "Yeah, you two scare me to death." There was no mistaking his sarcasm. After a penetrating stare, he uttered, "I stopped because when I make love to you, I want you to know it's me."

A tingling heat deluged her. She rose on unsteady legs and paced away from him to regain her equilibrium. She wanted to say that would never happen—she'd never make love to him knowing who he was—but it would sound too much like a challenge. She was feeling too vulnerable at the moment to throw down that particular gauntlet.

Prudently she changed the subject. "I didn't even know you were in town. When did you get here? Evan was supposed to be here, not you."

"I came in on the return flight he'd booked. Business is keeping him in Europe longer, and I was ready to come home. No sense in wasting nonrefundable airfare."

"But how could you have possibly thought I'd know that?"

"I've been out and about today. Plenty of people know I'm back in town."

"No one mentioned it to me."

"No? Well, take a look at this." He led her into the kitchen and gestured toward an array of items on the table: a bottle of champagne with a glittering "Welcome Home" card attached to its cork, a casserole with a ribbon and a card, a cake decorated with pink letters that spelled, "Waiting for You...Julie." A phone number comprised the lower border.

"Gifts from my, er, welcoming committee," he muttered.

Brianna surveyed the hometown offerings in dismay. When she found her voice, she stammered, "Y-you thought *I* was one of these women who...who throw themselves at you?"

His eyes lightened again. "You were the only one who actually threw herself at me."

"Ohh!" Curling her hands into fists, she rushed past him on her way out of the kitchen.

He grabbed her arm, turned her around. "Brianna—"

She shook loose of his grip. "I'd never in a million years debase myself by chasing after any man in such a disgusting way!"

"Oh, your way won...no contest." As her jaw lowered, he gave a mischievous half smile and lightly tugged on a tendril beside her ear. "Lighten up. You're taking this whole thing way too hard."

She glared at him. Of course Jake wouldn't see their intimacy as anything of significance. Life was a game to him, one big rollicking party. Rich, beautiful women around the globe indulged in his company as a kind of sport; the less rich ones pursued him as a vocational goal. From gossip about Jake Rowland, she'd learned one thing—he was a reckless adventurer incapable of taking a relationship seriously. Why should he? What could one woman possibly give him that the multitudes couldn't?

"You might not understand this, Jake," she finally managed to say with admirable control, "but unlike you, I don't take any sort of sexual involvement lightly."

He studied her for a considering moment. "I don't suppose you would. The only thing you'd take lightly would be my death." When she didn't argue, he went on, "But there's no reason to get hysterical over tonight's misunderstanding." His gaze clouded, and his voice lowered to a harsh whisper. "I mean, nothing went on between us that can't be forgotten...did it?"

The question lingered in the silence and echoed through her heart. *Did it?*

Oh, he was Jake, all right. There was no mistaking him now. Her stomach was clenching in that disturbing way, just because of his potent gaze and the question that burned like a laser within it. She wrenched herself away and looked about for her shoes. She had to get as far away from this man as possible.

"You didn't answer me, Brianna."

"Of course I can't just forget what happened. I owe it to Evan to tell him about it."

From the quality of Jake's silence, she knew she had surprised him. He followed her into the living room, then asked, "What exactly are you going to tell him?"

"The truth." She spotted her black high heels beside the hearth and stepped into them. Was he worried about what his brother would do when he found out?

When she glanced back at him, Jake was studying his watch. "This would be a good time to get in touch with him," he mused. "I have a number where you can reach him now."

"Now? You think I should call him *now*?"

He shrugged. "Might as well. That way I'll be here to back you up. We could, ah, face him together."

The idea of explaining their recent intimacy to Evan with Jake listening in—and adding his version of the event, no doubt—suddenly sounded less than wise. She got the distinct impression, though, that the prospect appealed immensely to Jake. "I'll call him later." She snatched her coat from the chair where she'd thrown it.

"That reminds me. Evan gave me a couple of letters before I left. Asked me to mail them when I got to the States." Jake reached past her and opened the coat closet. "One was addressed to you."

"To me?" she said in surprise.

"And one to his secretary."

She waited in curiosity while he retrieved letters from the pocket of his overcoat. Why would Evan send her a letter when he'd see her soon? As his human resources director, she often dealt with him, but usually in person, on the phone or through E-mail. She couldn't remember the last time he'd sent her a letter.

Jake handed her an envelope. Curiously, she opened it.

Dear Brianna:

Business will keep me abroad for a while. I've enjoyed our time together, but I feel it would be best to return our relationship to its former footing. I've suspected for some time that you might regret our romantic involvement. I wouldn't want to lose you as a friend.

I promise that our relationship will in no way affect your career, just as it hasn't in the past. I look forward to seeing you when I return. Yours in friendship,

Evan

Stunned, she lifted her eyes from the page in an unfocused daze. She'd lost him!

"What's wrong?" Jake asked, watching her.

"Nothing." Her mind reeled from the blow.

"Is it something about work?"

"No, no. It's personal." She folded the letter into a small square and tucked it into the pocket of her coat, which she'd draped over her arm.

"Are you sure you don't want to call Evan? Talk over the problem? I'll dial him up right now. We can also tell him about how you mistook me for him."

"No!" She grabbed at the lapels of his robe and gazed

up at him imploringly. "No, *please*, Jake. I...I don't want to tell him, and I don't want you to, either." Realizing how desperate she sounded, she released his lapels, smoothed them down in absent distraction, then became aware of the warm muscled chest beneath the robe. With a gasp, she snatched her hands away.

He cocked a brow, a disquieting twinkle in his eyes.

She lifted her chin and strove for dignity. "I've changed my mind about Evan's needing to know." Her pride had suffered enough without disclosing her humiliating error.

"I don't know," Jake ruminated, rubbing his chin, "He *is* my brother. Wouldn't want him to think I was moving in on his woman. Might be better to come clean right away."

Aware that Jake would sooner or later find out that Evan had broken up with her, Brianna swallowed a great big lump of pride. "I'm not *his woman* anymore. He wrote in the letter that he wants to be just friends." Anguished that she'd lost him through her own foolishness, she turned blindly toward the door and fumbled to put on her coat.

Jake took the coat from her and held it open. She allowed him to help her into it—a suave, gentlemanly gesture—but somehow he made it seem intimate, guiding her arms into the sleeves, lifting her hair from beneath the collar, fitting the coat snugly around her. "My brother's a damned fool," he muttered, fastening the top button.

"Don't talk about him that way," she whispered brokenly. "We had a fight before he left. It was my fault."

"And that's why you came over here tonight," he softly surmised, closing the next button, "wanting to make up after your fight. Wearing that sexy dress..." His fingers paused in their work, "And that lacy black underwear..." His gaze met hers, his voice roughened. "Kissing me like there's no tomorrow. Smelling good enough to eat."

The warmth sizzled through her again, revitalizing memories of all the things he'd done to her....

"Just forget about all that," she choked.

He slanted his head and frowned. "And what if I don't?"

She had to protect herself from these whispers of his, these heated gazes that dissolved her ability to think. He was a celebrated master at seduction—an international playboy. She couldn't allow herself to forget that, just because she suddenly longed for him to kiss her again.

"What are you doing here, anyway?" she cried, pushing his hands away from the coat button he still held. As she fastened it herself, she added for good measure, "This is Evan's apartment, not yours."

"It's both of ours. That's one thing about being a twin. There's a lot of sharing that goes on."

She looked up at him quickly. "You'd better not be referring to me."

His eyes clouded again to a deep smoky blue. "I wouldn't share you with anyone."

Her throat tightened with sudden, inexplicable emotion, and she found she couldn't break away from his solemn stare. "I have to go." She edged her way toward the door.

"Brianna, you're better off without Evan."

"That's not for you to say."

"He's not your type, and you're not his."

"You don't know anything about our 'types.'"

"No? Well, if it's so damned good with Evan," he taunted, drawing close enough that the fragrance of his hair and the feel of his breath against her face made her heart turn over, "then why, when you were trembling in my bed, did you say you didn't know it could be that way?"

Heat washed over her face, her neck, her entire body. He had no right to ask that. It was too personal a thing for him to know—that she'd never, in all her life, experienced the depth of pleasure he'd given her. He'd only find some way to use the admission against her...like mentioning it to Evan, or maybe to someone in town.

There was only one way she knew to insure against that. "I said it because I thought you were Evan and wanted you to feel special." With desperation, she drove the point home. "I felt sorry for you. I thought you were having a bad night."

"A bad night!"

"If you must know," she said in a scalding whisper, "I was faking it."

He grabbed the front of her coat and dragged her even closer, his face nearly touching hers. "If I didn't know that you were lying through those delectable—and talented—lips of yours, my feelings might be hurt."

She couldn't stand it—she pulled away and swung at him.

He caught her wrist. "Can this be the girl who boycotted football because she was against violence?"

With deep mortification, she realized he had a point. She had always deplored violence of any kind, and had campaigned vigorously against it. But she still wanted to slap him! How was it that Jake Rowland could undermine her innermost values? That, she realized, was the danger of him.

She ground out through clenched teeth, "I boycotted football because you were the quarterback."

"Don't think I didn't know that."

"I wish you hadn't come home. I hope you don't stay long."

A muscle tightened in his jaw, but he replied lightly enough, "If that isn't just like a woman. Tell you they love you to get you into bed, then treat you like dirt once they're satisfied."

She drew in a deep hissing breath. "Don't flatter yourself. I wouldn't want you in my bed...and I wasn't satisfied!"

"I think you were."

"Go to hell." She made a move for the door.

He blocked her way and raised an inquiring brow. "Does this mean I don't get *my* turn?"

She stared at him for one blank moment. "Your turn?"

"I saw to your sexual needs," he pointed out in a tone of patient reasoning. "So, uh...when do you see to mine?"

Her mouth bunched and her hands convulsed into fists. To stop herself from attempting another swing at him, she flung open the door and clattered down the steps, uttering the same vow she always took whenever Jake Rowland came to town: to keep a huge safety buffer between him and her for however many torturous days he'd be in the vicinity.

She fervently hoped those days would be few.

THE MOMENT JAKE HAD closed the door, he rammed his fist into its solid oak panels. The urge to punch something, anything, had been building up steadily since she'd called him Evan.

The door remained intact. His hand throbbed. He was glad. Maybe, just maybe, the pain would keep his mind off the woman he'd just chased away with his mouth.

He'd known better than to talk to her about Evan. He'd known better than to tease her or taunt her, or lose all perspective, all trace of common sense, when she looked at him with those distrustful hazel eyes that turned to a sultry golden green whenever he came too close.

She still wanted Evan.

Why had he believed, even for a second, that it might be otherwise? And why the hell did he care? All during his flight home, he'd sworn that this time he'd wouldn't let Brianna Devon get under his skin. He wouldn't get caught up in their game again—wouldn't start obsessing about ways to provoke her, no matter how badly she provoked him.

He hadn't expected that provocation to include showing up on his doorstep looking like a temptress, her hair a shiny sweet-smelling cloud, her whisper a warm invitation. *I've had time to think, while you were gone. I'm ready to make love to you.* The memory of that moment flushed through him with a sensual heat.

His hand would have to hurt a hell of a lot more to make him stop thinking about her tonight. Angry with himself, he strode to the kitchen where he wrapped some ice in a towel and crushed every damn cube into a fine powder. He'd hold the ice pack around his hand for the rest of the evening and concentrate on the cold and the pain.

And he'd sleep on the couch. He wouldn't go anywhere near his bed, where the memories would be the strongest. *I didn't know it could be this way*, she'd whispered. Again the heat poured through him. Nothing she could say or do would make him believe that she hadn't meant those words. Because after all his worldly experience, he had felt exactly the same way. He hadn't known that just holding and kissing a woman could make him damn near delirious.

Cursing, he threw the ice pack in the sink, grabbed a bottle of Jack Daniels from the cabinet and stalked into the living room, intent on drinking himself into forgetfulness. But as he uncapped the bottle and sank down onto the sofa, he remembered how she'd looked sitting there in the chair, her hair all wild from their tussle in bed, her lips a smooth natural pink and a little swollen from his kisses.

He'd wanted to take her back to bed.

Why the hell should he want her so much? She wasn't a devastating beauty. He hadn't even thought her particularly pretty the first time he saw her, back in high school.

She'd just been a mousy little girl hanging around with his brother. Evan was the president of some club, she was its vice-president. Evan wrote for the school newspaper, she edited it. He ran for a post, she managed his campaign. They did homework together at his house, planned their strategies beside his swimming pool, researched their projects on his family computer. Evan had considered her a friend, a pal. But Jake had known even then that she'd had a crush on Evan. He saw it in the way she looked at him.

And it really irked Jake. Especially because she refused to pay even one iota of attention to *him*. She never laughed at his jokes, never appreciated his fine wit... Hell, she never even pretended to like him.

It made him want to force her attention away from Evan and center it squarely on himself, by any method available. Rile up her passions, whatever passions he could possibly rile up, until she was forced to deal with him one-on-one.

Their relationship had somehow evolved into an ongoing public spectacle. Her attitude made it clear to everyone in school and in town that she considered him, Jake Rowland, to be inferior to his brother and beneath her standards.

Which of course, forced him to save face. He had to either win her over for all to see, or engage her in a battle that threatened *her* public image. At the debonair age of sixteen, he'd only managed the latter.

He'd teased her, heckled her, tricked her and generally made a nuisance of himself. The entire school had come to expect it of him. Like dropping a cricket down her back, then offering to recapture it. Hiding her book bag in the boys' locker room and daring her to find it. Toppling her occasional boyfriends headfirst into trash cans...all in the spirit of fun, of course.

His friends had begun to rib him about his devilment of the quiet little girl who shared her smiles with everyone but him. His girlfriends had begun to resent the time he spent dreaming up ways to plague her.

But that was in the past. He'd grown beyond the guerilla tactics he'd employed in high school. He now knew a good deal more about how to entice a woman. She wouldn't stand a chance against him now, if he set his mind to overcoming her defenses and wearing down her resistance.

Firmly Jake reminded himself of his resolve to leave Brianna alone. He no longer needed to prove himself in anyone's eyes...and he certainly didn't need her to satisfy his sexual needs. There was a world full of women out there, only too happy to cater to him.

So why did some fuse go off deep inside his chest every time he saw her, blowing his cool sky-high, making him say and do things to provoke her?

The answer, he supposed, was obvious. She was the woman he couldn't have. The one who got away. The challenge of the chase, the lure of the forbidden, the grass looking so lush and green on the other side of the hill.

He'd never been able to resist a challenge.

Tipping back the Jack Daniels bottle, he took a throat-burning swig. In the late night silence, broken only by the hiss of heat escaping the red hot embers, her accusation whispered through him like a demon. *How could you deceive me like that? You took your brother's place in bed with me!*

Guilt, he realized then, was a relative thing.

He honestly hadn't known she thought he was Evan, especially when she'd first waltzed in the door. He'd been thunderstruck that she'd come to welcome him home. But when a gift of that magnitude falls into a man's lap... When manna from heaven rains down on a starving wanderer... How could a question *not* form within the human heart?

It had seemed too good to be true. When she'd declared her age-old love, he'd suspected that something might not be quite right. But the moment that doubt had entered his head, he'd zapped it right back out. He'd indulged instead in the gratifying possibility that she had been secretly wanting him all those years—and in the sheer sexual pleasure of finally having her.

He'd always imagined she'd taste like heaven.

Now, he knew.

Nothing could have stunned him more—not even a bullet to the chest—than when she'd called him Evan. Which, when all was said and done, proved his innocence. Didn't it?

With a damning curse, he hurled the liquor bottle into

the fireplace. It shattered against the gray stones of the hearth, the fire hissing, then leaping erratically.

Who was he trying to kid? He was guilty as hell. He'd wronged her in the lowest, most despicable way known to man, then tried to pin his innocence on a technicality. No, he hadn't been one-hundred-percent sure that she'd mistaken him for Evan. But then, neither had he risked asking.

With elbows resting on outspread knees, he plowed his fingers through his hair. He had to make it up to her. He had to bury the hatchet, smoke the peace pipe.

He would not, under any circumstances, behave with anything less than chivalry toward her. He would not wonder just how deep her emotions toward his brother ran or how intimate their relationship had grown. He certainly wouldn't try to get her back in his own bed and finish what they'd started...make her cry out *his* name instead of Evan's....

Blowing out a steady breath, Jake rose from the sofa and plodded toward the den. He had to get her off his mind. Switching on the computer, he keyed in the password Evan had given him and scrolled through information about the company his brother ran.

As columns of figures flashed by him on the screen, Jake found himself taking comfort in the fact that Brianna hadn't known the circumstances that kept Evan in Paris. Obviously they hadn't been close enough for him to divulge the problem to her. And it was a serious problem—serious enough that Jake had spent the past two days dealing with French law enforcement, international attorneys and Interpol on his brother's behalf.

Ludicrous though it was, Evan had become implicated in an embezzlement—computer fraud against one of their largest overseas customers. He was being "asked" not to leave France until the investigation cleared him of suspicion.

Evan *would* be cleared, Jake felt sure. He'd never knowingly involve himself in theft or anything even vaguely shady. But the embezzlement, perpetrated from within the Rowland Insurance Company, created internal problems.

Even more surprising than the crime itself: his grandfather had asked Jake to help them out with their corporate difficulties.

That had been a shock. He'd thought he would be the last one his grandfather, the chairman of the board, would turn to for help. Nearly a decade ago, the old man had forbidden him to set foot in the family home because Jake had refused to work at the Rowland businesses and live under his thumb.

He'd live under *nobody's* thumb. If there was one thing Jake needed, it was freedom to go and do as he pleased. To keep two steps ahead of the rich man's curse—the boredom that sucked the color out of life when things got too easy.

Looking back, he was glad that he'd opted to strike out on his own. It had been tough at first, but he'd made a go of it, working abroad as a troubleshooter for major corporations—a kind of corporate doctor, diagnosing the problems of ailing companies and prescribing to their CEO's the cure. He hadn't lost a patient yet.

His grandfather obviously knew this, although Jake hadn't spoken to the old man since his banishment and hadn't told anyone else from home about his work. The very nature of it required discretion. Corporations paid big bucks to hide their problems from the world. Even his twin brother knew little about his consulting business. His wily old grandfather must have kept tabs on him all that time.

What did Cy Rowland have up his sleeve?

Jake supposed he'd learn the old man's reasons for calling on him soon enough. Probably Sunday. He'd been invited to dinner at his grandfather's house, the house Jake had once considered home.

He'd turned down that dinner invitation. They'd meet instead at a restaurant. Neutral ground.

As he scanned the personnel files on the computer screen, a name jumped out at him: *Brianna Devon*. He'd known that she held some position in the firm, but he hadn't known exactly which position. A slow smile spread across his face as he read her title.

So, she thought she could run away from him again, did she? Thought she could keep him at her usual distance? Ms. Brianna Devon had a surprise coming her way. As director of human resources, she'd be his right-hand man.

With his good cheer amazingly restored, he stretched his muscles, whistled a tune and headed for bed. Yes, bed. Not the couch. Maybe he wouldn't mind the memories of her there quite as much as he'd thought.

As he delved beneath the covers, the subtle scent of her surrounded him, bringing back every kiss, every groan. He allowed himself to savor the erotic heat.

And when he finally slept, he dreamt of wandering through the desert, hunger tearing at his stomach, when suddenly manna floated down from the heavens. He reached for it, his mouth watering with the need for food. But as he scooped it up, the manna turned to snow.

From the heavens came a scalding feminine whisper, all too familiar. "I was faking it!"

3

AFTER A RESTLESS WEEKEND during which Brianna tried to forget her humiliation of Friday night, Monday dawned bright and mild for mid-October in Ohio. Briskly she strode down the red brick sidewalks of Main Street, past awning-shaded shops of the historic village, struggling to restore her peace of mind before reaching the office.

Her breakup with Evan wasn't the worst that could happen, she told herself, nor was it necessarily permanent. He'd concluded that her reluctance to make love meant that she regretted dating him. She'd written an answer to his letter the previous night to explain how wrong he was. Surely they'd mend the rift when he came home.

Even her humiliating experience with Jake wouldn't affect her too much. They hadn't actually made love. But a deep, tingling warmth washed through her as she remembered how very close they'd come.

Resolutely she pushed the memory aside, assuring herself that her career was the important thing. As long as her career was going well—which it was—she'd be fine. Her income, her independence, her place in this warm little community she'd come to call home—all were secured by her career. Nothing could matter more.

She rounded a corner and approached the Rowland Insurance Company. Set a street behind the shops and diners of Main Street, the brick building had been designed to blend in with the historic ambience.

The charming old village, built around the Ohio & Erie canal business, had fallen on hard times when the canals closed. Surrounded only by Amish farmland, it had stood virtually vacant until the Rowland Insurance Company opened. As the business grew, so did Pleasantville.

With pride in the company and in the town, Brianna entered through the double glass doors. Inhaling the rich scent of leather furniture, rosewood desks and coffee, she made her way down the wide central corridor. At the last alcove on the left, she unlocked her office. In this small paneled sanctuary, she would build and control her future.

Cheered by the thought, she switched on the fluorescent light and hung up her coat, glad that Evan wouldn't be back for a few days. She wasn't ready for a confrontation.

Taking from her purse the letter she'd written to him, she dropped the envelope marked *confidential* into her interoffice mailbox. Evan's secretary would forward it to him unopened, regardless of where he happened to be.

She turned her attention to scheduling job interviews, scanning résumés and coordinating employee benefits. Around ten, she received a call from Maude Tupple, Evan's secretary, the least approachable employee in the firm.

"Good morning, Ms. Devon. I've just received a call from Cy Rowland's secretary."

At the mention of the chairman of the board—Evan's grandfather, son of the corporation's founder—Brianna sat straighter in her chair. "Yes?"

"You're expected at his office on Mulberry Street for a meeting around noon. He'll supply the lunch."

"I'm expected at his office?" repeated Brianna blankly. She'd never been singled out by anyone above Evan before. "Do you know who else is invited?"

"Just you. And, uh, me."

That surprised her even more. She'd been expecting to hear names of executives. What could the meeting be about? It had to be about Evan. Why else would the chairman of the board want to meet with his secretary?

Anxiety curled through Brianna. Something big was up. Something regarding Evan. The news might not be good.

FROM A HANDSOME STONE building on the town square, Cyrus Rowland ruled not only the Rowland Insurance Company but its highly diversified parent conglomerate. The conference room to which Brianna was ushered did not disappoint her; the gleaming conference table, leather chairs, a high ornate ceiling, original artwork on textured walls, all befitting the chairman of the board.

Cy Rowland radiated the charisma of those comfortable with power: his dark suit and tie, quietly expensive; his gold cufflinks, tie pin and ring, inset with dark rubies; his snow-white hair, glinting with a natural splendor. But it was his eyes that held her—beneath the snowy crests of his eyebrows, they were the same deep blue as his two grandsons.

"Ms. Devon, Ms. Tupple, I'd like you to meet our board members." From the far end of the table, he gestured toward the three men and two women, all in their sixties or seventies. The presence of the board members surprised Brianna. She hadn't been expecting a board meeting. In his deep rumbling voice, Cy made introductions. Brianna felt a tug of pride that she had been included in this exclusive group, and intense curiosity, as well.

"I've asked you two ladies to join us because of your long, excellent records with Rowland Insurance," said Cy, "and because my grandson Evan told me that you could be trusted to remain loyal and, er, discreet."

Brianna nodded a mute thanks.

He went on to talk about the history of the corporation, how his father and he had built it into an international conglomerate.

As he rambled on with passion for the subject, the door behind him opened and a broad-shouldered figure entered. For a surprised moment, Brianna thought it was Evan.

Evan, however, wouldn't attend a meeting or any business function in anything less than an Armani suit and tie. Evan wouldn't saunter in with his hands in his pockets and his hair too long and windblown. Evan wouldn't have been late.

This newcomer, dressed in casual trousers and a black crewneck sweater, the sleeves of which were pushed up his muscled forearms, lacked any sign of repentance for his tardy arrival as he settled into a chair at the opposite end of the long table from his grandfather—the chair nearest Brianna.

Her heart pounded in her ears as she stared at him. What was Jake doing here? He'd never before set foot in his family's corporate offices, as far as she knew. His name had never been linked to the business.

With growing unease, she struggled not to look at him. He hadn't glanced at her. His attention seemed properly centered on the speaker, although his chair was pushed out too far from the table, his arms negligently crossed, his powerful shoulders resting too low in the chair. He looked as if he were at home watching television.

"And that, ladies," said Cy, reclaiming her attention, "brings me to the point of this meeting. Rowland Insurance is the chief industry in this town. The local economy depends on our continued success. That success," he said, focusing on Brianna, "is going to depend largely on you."

She gazed back at the old man in puzzlement.

"We recently suffered a setback," he said. "Funds were embezzled from us and from our clients' accounts. Our chief financial officer manipulated the books and the computer system, then took off with the cash."

"Cassandra Jones?" she asked, stunned by the news.

"*If* that was her real name." The old man's voice vibrated with agitation. "She got away with millions."

A sick feeling lodged in Brianna's stomach. She never had trusted Cassandra, a willowy blonde with an Ivy League degree, who'd been hired by the former human resources director. She'd left the company on very short notice.

Brianna remembered Evan with sudden concern. How betrayed he must be feeling! "What's happened to Evan?"

"He's been detained in France," Cy muttered. "The theft was discovered by one of our French customers, a corporate client. Evan was called in to explain. He won't be free to leave until he's been cleared of suspicion."

"Suspicion!" Her worried gaze flew to Jake. Why hadn't he told her Friday night? He returned her regard with cool detachment, as if unaware of the importance this news held for her. "Surely they don't suspect Evan of embezzlement!"

Jake didn't comment, but Cy mumbled, "His password was used to gain access to the corporate accounts. He'll be cleared of all suspicion, I'm sure, by the time the French have finished the investigation." His voice grew more irate. "Meanwhile, we have to clear up problems here."

The old man's face had grown red, and he pulled a linen handkerchief from his pocket to blot his neck. "Funds were shifted via computer—not only from our bank accounts but from *customers'*, using our automatic draft system. We've paid back the deficiencies already found and blamed it on computer errors, but there may be more."

Brianna thought of the recent conflicts between departments over "errors" in the computer system.

"It'll take more to fix the problem than just pumping money back into the accounts," Cy said. "It's a matter of how to apply the money and where. We haven't even begun to figure out the details of the theft. That will take some time and analysis." In a morose grumble, he added, "Besides using Evan's computer password, the embezzler forged his signature on documents. Left him holding the bag."

Fear welled up in Brianna. Would Evan be held responsible for the theft?

A steely look entered Cy's eyes. "If word gets out that our problems are anything other than computer errors, Evan could become the target of a criminal investigation here, as well. A panic would start among the customers, the employees and the stockholders. We could be sued. The state could pull our insurance license. An insurance company sells *trust*, above anything else. Our customers trust that we're dealing honestly with them, and that when the rough times hit we'll be there. A whisper of doubt about our integrity, our capability or our stability, and Rowland Insurance becomes a threat to the entire conglomerate."

As the scope of the problem sank in, Brianna clenched her fists in her lap. She couldn't stand the thought of Evan being investigated for embezzlement. And if a scandal weakened Rowland Insurance, her very world could suffer a devastating blow.

In the chair to her left, Maude sat as white-faced as Brianna felt. Maude's career seemed to be her life. She'd no doubt do everything in her power to help.

"What can we do, sir?" Brianna asked.

The white-haired chairman of the board leaned back in his seat. "You can help keep things running smoothly while the problems are being resolved. If our contacts at Interpol have difficulty finding the embezzler and proof of Evan's innocence, he may be detained for quite some time."

Her heart fell at that prospect.

"Meanwhile," said Cy, "I forbid any communication between Evan and anyone in the corporation. His phone lines may be tapped. His mail may be intercepted. Any communication could be distorted into 'incriminating' evidence. At the very least, word of this fiasco could leak out to the press. I've paid dearly to try to prevent that."

Brianna thought about the letters Jake had given her Friday night from Evan. He hadn't been able to mail them!

Cy continued, "We'll need a chief executive officer while Evan is gone. The trouble is, a change in CEO's will signal a problem. Make people take a closer look— stockholders, employees, customers, state officials. The last thing we need right now is scrutiny."

Brianna chewed on her lower lip. How could someone new step in as CEO without anyone knowing about it?

"Tell me, ladies," said Cy in a suddenly amiable voice, "have you met my other grandson, Jake?"

As she reeled from the sudden change in subject, Maude said, "Well, yes, but it's been a long time." The secretary cast a shy glance at Jake. "In fact, at first I thought..." her thin cheeks brightened with splotches "...I thought he was Mr. Rowland. Uh, *Evan* Rowland, that is."

A smile lifted the corner of Jake's firm, wide mouth. "A common mistake," he murmured. His blue-eyed gaze shifted to Brianna. "People I've known for years confuse us."

She felt her own embarrassment rise. He was, of course, referring to Friday night. She looked away from him, hoping he'd say no more. Ever.

"Yes, they're virtually identical," said Cy, his voice strangely emphatic. "Which brings me to my plan."

"Your plan?" repeated Brianna, highly aware that Jake continued to watch her—like a cat about to pounce on a canary. Why the devil was he here, anyway?

"Jake has agreed to help us out of this crunch," Cy announced. "He's going to be your new CEO."

Brianna's eyes widened.

"No one but us will have to know," continued Cy. "The board will grant Jake the legal authority, but with Maude handling his paperwork the other employees need not be told. As far as the world is concerned, Evan hasn't left."

Brianna gaped at the chairman in dismay as the others murmured in pleased agreement. Only she saw the madness in the scheme; only she sat dazed by the bomb that had just exploded. "With all due respect, sir," she began, "Jake grew up in this town. I realize he's been gone for a while and that most of our employees wouldn't know him, but some of them do! He may look like Evan, but he certainly doesn't *act* like Evan or *dress* like Evan. He doesn't know how Evan interacts with people at work...."

"That's another reason we'll need your help, Ms. Devon," said Cy. "Evan recommended you for the job of preparing Jake for his role. He said you and Maude know more about his daily habits and relationships than anyone else. I'll be counting on you for that."

She stuttered a reply that Cy took as affirmative. Obviously pleased with the meeting thus far, he called his secretary in and instructed that lunch be served.

Conversation broke out all around the conference table. In pained disbelief—surely the legendary Cy Rowland couldn't believe that an inexperienced playboy could take over the corporate reins of Rowland Insurance?—Brianna roused herself out of her stupor to peer at Jake.

It was as bad as she feared—that disconcerting twinkle was back in his sea blue gaze. And that gaze rested on her.

"Tell me, Mr. Rowland," she finally managed to say to Jake, loud enough for his grandfather to overhear, "do you have any experience as a CEO?"

"No," he admitted. "But everyone has to start somewhere. Beats the hell out of the mail room."

Cy grunted a laugh as if he'd heard a good joke, then turned back to his conversation with those seated at his end of the table. Board members chatted among themselves and with Maude, while servers scurried about setting sandwiches and drinks in front of everyone.

Jake winked at Brianna.

Through stiff lips, she kept her voice low enough this time for only him to hear. "Do you know anything at all about insurance?"

"Not much. But I have some corporate experience as a consultant."

"A consultant? What kind of consultant?" She could just imagine...!

"Are you interviewing me for this job, Ms. Devon?"

Though he hadn't changed his tone or expression, the chastisement came across clearly. She was being presumptuous, questioning the chairman's decision. She should drop the subject. Unfortunately she couldn't. In a heated whisper, she asked, "What makes you think you can run an insurance company, even for a few months?"

"A well-developed sense of self. And of course, the moral support of loyal employees like you."

Her mouth went dismally dry, and she reached for her glass of water.

"You don't have to go along with this," he reminded her. "Speak up now and put an end to it. Let the chips fall where they may. If worse comes to worst, Evan will just have to face the consequences of his mismanagement."

Brianna bristled. "He didn't mismanage anything. He was taken in by a professional thief. A computer hacker."

"If the scandal breaks," continued Jake, "the customers will move their money to safer ground. Stockholders will face their losses, even if it takes everything some of them have. The media will publish the lurid details, even if they have to make some up. By the way, that embezzler...I've heard she's young and pretty. Is she?"

When Brianna didn't reply, Jake shrugged. "Just wondered. Because if she is, it would add the right flavor to send the media into a feeding frenzy. A handsome young CEO and his pretty blond financial officer." He cocked a brow at her. "You *do* consider Evan handsome, don't you?"

She tightened her mouth. A totally irrelevant question...and a loaded one, as he well knew, since he was Evan's identical twin. "You've made your point," she mumbled. *Of course* the press would endow the incident with sexual overtones. *Of course* that would upset her to no end.

"I didn't say I wouldn't go along with the plan, Jake," she said, anguished at her lack of options. "You know I'll do whatever it takes to protect Evan and the company."

He studied her for a long moment. "You called me Mr. Rowland before. Is that what the employees call Evan?"

"Most of them."

"Then, let's set the ground rules." The humor had left his voice; the amused glint vanished from his stare. "No matter who calls me by my brother's name, I won't take it from you. Don't ever call me Evan."

Held by the severity of his gaze—and by the memory of the last time she'd called him Evan—she heard a slight *thump*, and realized she had knocked over her water glass. The icy liquid splashed down into her lap. With a cry, she reached for a napkin. As she dabbed at the saturated front of her suit, Jake leaned toward her and said in a hoarse whisper, "That's not salt water, by any chance...is it?"

Salt water.

A long ago memory from their high school days sizzled into her bloodstream, and her breath caught near the base of her throat. Without looking at him, she murmured a choked apology and excused herself from the table.

She knew exactly what glint would be in his eyes now.

SHE'D WANTED TO run away from him again, Jake knew, but she'd returned to the table with her head held high and her poise restored, although her beige suit remained water stained.

And though she sat close enough to him for a whisper to caress her ear, close enough for her perfume to tease his senses, she resolutely ignored him.

His grandfather hadn't yet adjourned the meeting, and the ever so correct Ms. Brianna Devon wasn't about to chance alienating the chairman of the board just because water had soaked through to her skin and the obnoxious bastard sitting beside her had resurrected a prickly memory.

He shouldn't have done it. She was having a hard enough time worrying about her beloved Evan and his company, whose fate would now rest in his hands. So why, then, when he'd sworn to keep peace with her, had he brought up the touchy subject of salt water?

Jake picked up his pastrami sandwich and admitted the truth to himself: he'd said it to see if she remembered. No doubt about it—she remembered that day as clearly as he, that hot September afternoon ten-plus years ago.

He'd pulled a prank on her that morning during her home ec class. Just before her demonstration on how to grill hamburgers—a feast to which she'd invited some jerk from the swim team—Jake had paid a friend to toss popcorn kernels into the charcoal. He'd heard later that the popcorn had exploded beneath her hamburgers with perfect timing.

That afternoon, when football practice had ended, he'd slung his helmet aside and taken a swig from his icy water bottle, only to spit out the vile-tasting stuff. Someone had salted his water. That's when he saw the handwriting in black marker on the bottle: *Salt to go with your popcorn.*

It was the first time she'd ever retaliated.

He'd spotted her then, sitting in the grass beyond the bleachers, pretending to read a book while secretly watching his reaction. He reacted, all right. He stalked toward her like a charging defensive linebacker, armed with his sabotaged water bottle. Her eyes grew wide. She jumped to her feet, dropped her book and took off running.

He easily tackled her behind the bleachers, pinned her down in the fragrant summer grass and locked her arms above her head with just one of his hands.

Breathless from the run, she struggled to break free, her yells little more than garbled yelps. No one was near enough to hear her, anyway. The old wooden bleachers and the late afternoon hour provided them a rare privacy.

He took his own sweet time dribbling that cold salt water all over her face, her neck, her blouse.

She had on one of those round-collared blouses that prim little schoolgirls wear. He hadn't known that the thin white cotton would cling to her skin when it got wet...and turn perfectly transparent.

Her breasts took him by surprise. Stunned him. He hadn't seen much of them before, other than in vague imaginings of what might lie beneath her prudish clothes. He saw them clearly now, round and pointed, with nipples dark and hardened beneath her lacy bra.

He felt himself hardening, too—quicker and fuller

than ever. He forced himself to look away from those nipples, those breasts, forced his free hand to clamp down on her arms instead of touching her the way he so wanted.

Water glistened in inviting droplets on her face, her neck, her lips.

"I like the way you made my water taste," he whispered against her ear. "In fact, I'm gonna lick up every drop I spilled." He tightened his hold on her and started at her jaw, beneath her ear, licking a wide, slow path up the side of her face—like he would a lollipop or a Popsicle or any other luscious treat that he couldn't get quite enough of.

She'd been laughing a little at first, out of nervousness more than fun, and yelling for him to quit. But he hadn't. And somewhere along the way, she'd stopped yelling and gotten quiet, and all they could hear was their breathing and their heartbeats and the lapping of his tongue over her skin.

He'd been teasing, just teasing. But by the time he got to her mouth, he'd forgotten why he'd started and knew only that he didn't want to quit.

But she was whispering something now. "Stop, Jake. Please stop!" A soft, trembling whisper, and when he pulled back to search her eyes, he saw a deep, dark struggle going on there. Her words were telling him no, but something in those eyes urged him on. Urged him to do what he wanted.

It took every ounce of his self-control to get off her. With his insides burning, he pulled her to her feet. Then he made some crack about having to watch his salt intake.

He'd been a witty bastard, though, hadn't he?

Keep it light. Always keep it light. His credo.

But he hadn't been able to forget how she'd looked, breathing slow and hard beneath him on that grass, or how she'd felt, her skin smooth and tender beneath his tongue. He tried to forget. He'd gone on plenty of dates with warm and willing girls, made love to a few of them. But he'd found himself pretending it was Brianna he was kissing, Brianna he was feeling...

Keep it light. If anyone could keep the emotional tone of a relationship light, he could. He'd mastered that survival skill at an early age. But his game with Brianna had taken a dangerous turn, and now involved something more than pride.

Something sexual.

He hadn't actually tasted her then, that September afternoon ten-plus years ago. The salt water had interfered. He hadn't tasted her until this past Friday night....

Desire, hot and swift, brought him out of his musings and back into the conference room, where his grandfather was extracting vows of cooperation from the women as they walked toward the door.

He was glad the meeting had been adjourned, glad Brianna was leaving. Because otherwise her resolve to ignore him would break down and she'd turn those expressive hazel eyes his way. He wasn't sure he could take that right now.

The memory of the saltwater incident was just too real to acknowledge without touching her.

LATER THAT AFTERNOON, Cy's corporate helicopter hovered in the gray sky above a hilly green golf course. Separated from the pilot by a soundproof Plexiglas wall, Cy pointed an arthritic finger and uttered in his usual gruff voice, "That's our new course. Evan had it built for executives and visiting clientele." As Jake surveyed the plush fairway below, Cy said, "We'll open it up to employees on special occasions." Pride sounded in his voice.

"Looks like the company's enjoyed a lot of growth," observed Jake.

"You're damn right, it has." Cy's gaze grew stern. "All that time you were having your fun, Evan was here building this company into what it is today."

Jake set his teeth in careful alignment, bracing himself. He'd known it would flare up sooner or later—the bitterness over his refusal to work at the family business.

Cy's voice shook as he sermonized, "Rowland Insurance grew by leaps and bounds under Evan's direction. I couldn't be any prouder of him. Ironic, isn't it, that the company's welfare now depends on you?" He shook his head. "If I had any other way of helping Evan, I'd take it."

Jake was careful not to react. A show of anger or pain would only add fuel to the old guy's fire. Jake had learned the unflattering truth the previous day at their Sunday dinner meeting—Cy hadn't called for his help because of his reputation as a corporate troubleshooter. The only reason he'd called him was because of his likeness to Evan. He simply needed his face. A front man.

"Just remember, boy—the money I'm willing to pay will keep you in women for quite some time. Just show up for work every day, keep your mouth shut and do what I tell you."

The muscles in Jake's jaw hardened. If Cy had been any other man, he'd have put him through the helicopter window. *Keep it light,* he reminded himself.

"And if the money isn't enough to make you see this thing through," Cy rasped, "do it for the family name. Or for your brother. He'd damn sure do it for you."

"You seem to have misunderstood our agreement, sir." Jake kept his tone amiable. "I didn't accept this job for my brother or for the family name. I'll bill the corporation for my services, just as I would any other client. This is business. Just business."

Cy's blue eyes glittered like agates as he stared at Jake in affront.

"And about my showing up for work every day," Jake said evenly, "I set my own schedule. Work at my own pace. Go where the job takes me."

Bushy white brows drew together over a frown.

Jake shot him a challenging stare. "And if you expect me to wait for your orders before I make a move, then you've hired the wrong man. I'll do what I can to pull the company through...but I'll do it my way. If you find you don't like my methods, you can always fire me."

They stared at each other in unblinking silence as the helicopter landed. Before disembarking, Jake paused. "I've got other commitments that'll keep me occupied until Friday. Consider that my first day on the job."

4

"RESERVE FRIDAY FOR ME. I'll need you all day." The message had been on her voice mail that Monday afternoon when she'd returned to her office. The deep resonance of Jake's voice had started her heart pumping a little too hard.

I'll need you all day. The message had been brief and uttered without inflection of any kind, yet Brianna responded with a secret rush of warmth, of dread, of anticipation. How could a simple message affect her so? He'd done the same to her at the conference table. *"That's not salt water, is it?"*

That particular memory had engulfed her like a steamy bath—Jake's strong, muscular body pressing hers down into the grass, his mouth hot against her skin, igniting a new, dangerous hunger within her. Which led her to remembering more recent encounters. Like last Friday night.

She couldn't allow herself to think that way about him!

Tuesday morning, Chloe called. Casually she mentioned that Jake had bought drinks for everyone at the corner pub the previous evening to celebrate his last night in town. A young blond waitress, an older brunette and Chloe herself had accompanied him to the airport, where he'd kissed all three good-bye. Chloe had considered the evening great fun.

Just hearing about it annoyed the hell out of Brianna. Grudgingly she understood why he'd left with such fanfare—too many people had known he was in town. By making a spectacle of his departure, he could then return a couple days later as Evan, with Jake out of the picture.

Brianna wondered where he'd gone. She wondered *how* he'd kissed the women at the airport. Pecks on the cheek? She couldn't picture *that*. Slow and deep was more his style.

Thoughts of him tormented her throughout the week while she scanned résumés, checked references and scheduled performance reviews. She couldn't help wondering where he was. Why would he be out until Friday? How did he plan to make his entrance? And of course, the worst question of all, would his impersonation work?

To lessen her anxiety, she turned her attention even more than usual to her "venting" duty—lending an ear to troubled co-workers. Not an official part of her job, actually, but she considered it important nonetheless. They'd come to her, off the record, to talk about conflicts they faced. Long before she'd become director of human resources, co-workers had gravitated to her with their problems.

"She's wearing it again," an underwriter had whispered at the water cooler, speaking of her manager. "That cologne that gives us all headaches. She won't take a hint."

A sales rep had charged into Brianna's office to warn, "If Pete doesn't get off my back about those reports, I'll go over his head. Let the big wheels see the numbers I'm bringing in and have *them* decide how many reports I have to do."

A service manager stopped by to confide, "I don't know what to do with Ellie. She fell asleep in her chair, snoring! But she's been our receptionist for decades."

Brianna had given each her full attention. Sometimes that alone was enough to defuse the tension. At other times she tried to help with advice or a word in the right ear. She took pride in being the peacemaker, the arbitrator, the confidante to whom clerks and executives alike would turn.

Many squabbles lately centered around computer errors. Those errors, she realized, had probably been caused by the embezzler's manipulations.

Oh, Evan, how could you have allowed her to get away with the theft? Immediately she squelched that traitorous thought. Evan wasn't to blame. He'd had no way of knowing the embezzler's intentions. She wished she could talk to him, but she had no idea where he was and Cy had forbidden communication with him.

Friday, it seemed, arrived sooner than usual. She'd postponed her other obligations for the day and let it be known that she might be out of the office. By six-thirty on that crisp, clear morning, she was striding down the red-brick sidewalks of Pleasantville, annoyed that Jake hadn't called her to make arrangements.

But that was typical of Jake. If Evan had asked her to reserve the day, he would have called her long before now to make plans. She wasn't sure that Jake would even show up.

A familiar car whizzed by—Evan's elegant beige Mercedes. For a crazy hopeful moment, she wondered if he'd straightened out the complications in France and returned home. That hope, however, was painfully short-lived.

The sedan screeched to a halt on the narrow street,

then shifted into reverse and drove backwards—all the way down Main Street! She glanced in alarm for oncoming cars. The street, however, was vacant. Only a few pedestrians lingered on the sidewalks at this early hour.

The Mercedes stopped beside her, the tinted passenger window hummed as it lowered and a deeply tanned Jake Rowland flashed a brilliant smile at her from behind the wheel. "Mornin', Ms. Devon."

Raw masculine charisma radiated from him like an electromagnetic field. She felt the draw, an almost primal attraction, but she wouldn't succumb to it, not even with a courteous smile. Instead, she glanced around, hoping that no one had seen his little driving stunt. They'd know immediately that the driver couldn't be Evan.

Curious heads had turned, she noticed. Through stiff lips, she replied, "Good morning, Mr. Rowland."

"Hop in."

Her first impulse was to refuse. A ride from Jake had always meant trouble. Like the morning she'd missed the school bus and out of desperation accepted his offer to drive her. He'd taken off down country highways with his radio blaring. "Welcome to Hooky 101," he'd told her. Only when she'd threatened to jump from the car had he taken her to school. She'd missed her first two classes.

"Well?" he prompted, leaning on his forearms against the leather steering wheel. "Are you going to get in, or would you rather meet me at the office?"

That, she realized, would be a disaster. He wore a faded green sweatshirt, a leather jacket and jeans, his brown mane far too long and shaggy, his strong jaw shadowed with stubble. He looked wild, wicked and dangerous—like an outlaw, or a rebel, or a footloose mil-

lionaire with the world in his jeans pocket. The latter
scared her most of all.

Drawing a breath, Brianna opened the car door and
slid into the passenger seat. "Go," she ordered in a low,
emphatic tone, her tension mounting as she surveyed
the pedestrians on the sidewalks, hoping no one had noticed her climb into his car. She wouldn't want to stir up
questions about her absence from the office. "*Slowly*,"
she specified as he accelerated through town. "Evan
would never speed the way you do." She fastened her
seat belt and cast Jake a critical glance. "And you can't
go to the office dressed like that."

"You don't like my duds?"

She looked away from the playful sparkle in his vivid
blue eyes. He was taking this far too lightly, just as she'd
known he would. "Evan wears suits to work. And he
shaves. You look like you haven't touched a razor in
days."

"Not since Tuesday. But we're not going to the office."

She narrowed her gaze, and Jake's grin deepened the
vertical groove beside his mouth. With a quickening in
her midsection, Brianna asked, "Where are we going,
then?"

He turned down a side street and headed back the
way they'd come. "Someplace where we can be private."

A trill of alarm raced through her. She didn't want to
be anywhere private with Jake Rowland.

As if noticing her unease, he added, "You can fill me
in on some details before I go into the office. Advise
me."

She couldn't argue with that. But just how private a
place did he have in mind? "You could have called me. I

could have advised you over the phone—what to wear, where to meet me..."

"I was out of the country and not sure what time I'd get back."

"A call from the airport would've been better than none."

"Sorry. I'll remember that next time." He cast her a disarming smile, and she lapsed into uncomfortable silence. He turned down her street and pulled up in front of her bungalow. "I thought we'd start with your place."

"*My* place? Why?"

"Pictures."

"Pictures?"

"Yeah. You know, photographs of people you work with. You could put names to the faces. You probably have albums full of photos from office parties and picnics and whatnot. In high school you never went anywhere without your camera."

She gazed at him in some surprise—first, because his idea made so much sense, and second, because she hadn't realized he'd noticed her picture-taking back in high school. She felt absurdly pleased that he had. And that he remembered. "I do have a few photos of co-workers."

"Good. Get 'em."

In a more optimistic frame of mind, she trekked up the stone walkway to her front porch. She hadn't expected him to follow her; she assumed he'd wait in the car. But his car door slammed and footsteps kept pace with her.

"Mind if I grab a cup of coffee while you're looking for those photos?" His rough baritone came from close behind her as she unlocked her door. "I came straight from the airport. Just had time for a quick shower and change."

She pushed open the door and paused awkwardly inside. Allowing Jake Rowland into her home seemed a dangerous thing to do. He strolled past her with easy confidence, into her living room with its embroidered quilt on the sofa, braided throw rugs on the oak floor and crocheted doilies beneath the lamps. His towering broad-shouldered form seemed so alien here, so... invasive.

An odd reaction, she realized, since his identical twin had spent many evenings relaxing here with her. She'd never felt tense in her home with Evan. But then, Evan was so predictable. With him, she was safe. In control.

Not so with Jake.

"You *do* have coffee, don't you?"

With a start, she realized she'd been standing there gawking at him, as if she'd never seen a man within these walls before. "Yes, yes, of course," she replied, sounding a little too breathless. "In the kitchen, next to the coffeemaker. Do you know how to make it?"

"Yes, ma'am," he drawled, his voice soft, his eyes lingering on hers. "I know how to make it."

Anxiety—and something equally uncomfortable—seeped into her blood. Was she imagining the sensuality in those words, in that stare? Feeling suddenly warm, she turned away and unbuttoned her fleece-lined coat. Before she guessed his intentions, he helped her out of it, pulling the coat from her shoulders. Too vividly it reminded her of the previous Friday night...when he'd peeled every last scrap of clothing off her and carried her to his bed.

Did he plan to stay here in her home, alone with her?

"You'll need to get out of that suit," he said. His gaze meandered down the curves of her gray tailored jacket and slim black skirt. A tingling began beneath her skin.

What was he suggesting? Curtly she took the coat from him and hung it in the closet.

"Might as well slip into something more comfortable."

At that, her bottom lip curled in disdain. He hadn't even bothered to be original. Slip into something more comfortable. He'd been watching too many old movies!

She whirled to confront him, a stinging rebuke poised on her tongue. Her gaze locked with his—like bucks locking antlers for battle—and she noticed the expectant twinkle in his gaze. He'd meant to provoke her, she realized, and fully expected her to chastise him.

She wouldn't give him the satisfaction.

"Jeans," he said, his eyes bright with amusement. "And a sweatshirt, maybe, since we're not going to the office. We'll need at least a full day to prepare me for my role." He turned his back to her and sauntered toward her kitchen. The scoundrel. He knew she felt uncomfortable here with him, and he delighted in getting a rise out of her.

Locking herself in her bedroom, she slipped out of her suit and changed into jeans. Obstinately she chose a cranberry knit sweater instead of the prescribed sweatshirt. She had to exert control. She'd been charged with the task of turning Jake into Evan, and she meant to do just that.

Flipping through her photo albums, she found one with pictures of co-workers. His idea had been good— she'd identify people he'd run into at the office. But it would take much more than that to prepare him for his role. She also found her employee handbook and a set of training manuals.

With an armload she returned to the living room. Jake sat on the sofa with a cup of coffee between his large bronzed hands. Seeing him there reminded her again of Friday night, when he'd given her coffee after their interlude in bed. After he'd kissed her and touched her and worked her up into an orgasmic frenzy...

"Let's go into the kitchen," she said tersely. The sofa wouldn't be conducive to work.

"I hadn't planned on us staying here." He stood up. "I've rented a place to work for the day."

Warily she asked, "What kind of place?"

"You'll see. It's in the next county, so no one will disturb us or know we're together." He'd surprised her again with his foresight. What, she wondered, was behind it?

They drove an hour northwest, down hilly two-lane highways through Amish country, past neat farms and rolling woodlands bright with the crimsons, yellows and golds of autumn. Brianna made the most of their time by reading aloud from a training manual, tutoring him on insurance lingo.

She wasn't sure he was listening. He seemed distracted by every quaint Amish buggy and horse that clip-clopped along the highway, every sparkling expanse of river, every picturesque barn and hilltop that caught his eye.

Reining in her own wandering attention, she returned to the training manual. Today was a workday, and even though she was following Cy Rowland's orders to prepare Jake for his role, she felt guilty for enjoying the break from the office. Intent on putting in an honest day's work, she reprimanded Jake, "This is important for you to learn."

"I'm listening. But it's been years since I've driven these back roads. I can't help looking around." He stretched his muscles, as if just now rising from bed.

"Besides, I'm not awake yet. Didn't get much sleep on the flight back from Mexico."

"Mexico!" she exclaimed, again distracted in spite of herself. "What in heaven's name were you doing in Mexico?"

"Running across Xinantecatl." With a glance at her, he explained, "A dormant volcano. Ever been there?"

A volcano! He'd spent Tuesday, Wednesday and Thursday racing across a volcano? "No," she replied faintly, "not any time recently."

"Southwest of Toluca. At fifteen-thousand feet above sea level, the air's too thin for anyone to run very far or fast. I barely finished a mile. But that's all it took." He flashed a buoyant smile. "I won the bet."

A bet. He'd done it on a bet. His brother was being held captive by French authorities and his family's company was facing disaster, yet he'd found time to jog across a volcano. To win a bet.

She couldn't help asking, "Who bet you couldn't?"

"Ry Alexander. An old college buddy of mine. He and his wife, Sunny, happened to be vacationing near there."

The names rang a bell. Something to do with high society and big money. "You're not talking about *Ryan* Alexander, are you? *The* Ryan Alexander, of Alexander Computer Technologies?"

"You've heard of him?"

"Of course I've heard of him. Who hasn't? He and his wizards revolutionized cyberspace."

"Yeah, that's Ry. A computer nut from way back. Just doesn't know which side of a wager to bet on." Again he gave a victorious grin, much like the ones she remembered from high school after his football triumphs.

How different their lives were, his and hers! His triumphs meant cocky grins and bragging rights. Hers meant a roof over her head and a community in which to set down roots. She'd rarely left Ohio, while the world itself was his playground. She planned her life around her work. He lived minute by minute, not having to work at all. Not having to strive or plan. Or care.

It frightened her, thinking of him in that limitless way. The image came to mind of a helium balloon she'd been handed as a child—bright and glistening in the sun. She'd lost hold of its string and it rose from her hand, far above her reach. Aimlessly it drifted, higher and higher, twirling with every playful breeze, until it was just a speck in the sky. And then...gone.

Did he ever get lonely, she wondered of Jake, scaling the boundless heights, twirling with every playful breeze?

Shaking herself out of the melancholy she'd somehow drifted into, she decided it was up to her to bring him down to earth and anchor him for as long as this project took. Once again, she began to read from the manual.

Jake interrupted her by stopping at an Amish pie stand, filling the car with the fragrance of cinnamon and spice, making her mouth water. He also bought fragrant, warm homemade bread, fresh deli meats and coffee.

When he returned to the driver seat, she railed at him, "This is a workday, Jake, not a vacation. If anyone is going to believe that you're Evan, you'll have to at least learn some insurance terminology, clean up your appearance and adopt a more serious attitude."

He frowned as he shifted the car into gear. "You seem to doubt that I can play Evan."

"*Play* Evan?" she repeated. So it was just a game to him. "We're going to need a major miracle." She might have been imagining it, but she thought she saw his hands tighten on the steering wheel.

"Since you're the expert on the subject of my twin," he replied flatly, "go ahead. Transform me."

"Okay," she said with a nod. "Stop at a barbershop in the next town. You need a cut and shave."

"I can shave at home."

"Someone from work might see you when we return to town this afternoon. They'd know that you weren't Evan. Evan always keeps himself well-groomed. Even on his days off, he maintains the image of a community leader."

"Should I genuflect any time soon? Fall to my knees, sing a few hymns?"

She ignored his sarcasm, insisted he stop at a barbershop and ushered him to the barber chair. The beefy man with an overgrown mustache grunted and went to work with his shears. Jake watched through the mirror in stoic silence.

"Shorter in the back," Brianna judged, secretly hating to see the thick, glossy brown waves fall to the floor. "It shouldn't touch his collar," she justified. "Oh, and a little more layered on the sides."

"I'm not shipping off to boot camp," Jake muttered as the barber cut away inches from his tousled mane.

"We want a neat, groomed look," she explained. "One that shouts, 'Executive.'" The barber sent Jake a commiserating glance—one that groaned, "Women."

When he'd finished, Jake looked much more like Evan. Except, of course, for the faded jeans, sweatshirt and brown leather jacket...the subtle arrogance in his nonchalant manner...the devil-may-care glint in his sea blue eyes...

Would anyone believe he was Evan? Incredible to think that *she* had, last Friday night. But his hair had been wet from a shower, she remembered, and his personality muted by the shock of her unexpected appearance. How else could she have confused the two?

She paused on the curb outside the barbershop as Jake stepped down onto the street. With a hand on his shoulder, she stopped him and examined his profile. "Evan wears a more definite part," she reflected, giving in to the urge to touch his newly shorn hair. The silken strands flowed through her fingertips as she rearranged a critical lock here and there. "Yours seems to have more golden highlights," she murmured. "We might have to—"

"Forget it." With a smooth quarter turn, he faced her, almost eye level and much too near. "How's my shave?" he whispered. Then he nuzzled his chin against the side of her neck.

With a gasp she flexed her shoulder to fend him off, trapping his jaw against her collarbone. His nearness submerged her in sensation: the virile scent of his hair and skin, the slightly abrasive rub of his jaw, the warmth of his breath as it steamed against her throat.

He drew back only far enough to read her eyes. "Think it's close enough?"

Thoroughly shaken, she pulled away, gave his solid chest an ineffectual shove and stalked past him to the car. She felt dazed and rattled and miffed at herself as well as him. She'd had no business playing with his hair. She should have known better than to touch Jake Rowland at all.

But if truth be told—which it never would—she *had* been thinking about how his shaven face would feel against her skin. Actually, she *knew* how it would feel. She'd felt it last Friday night.

Sliding into the passenger seat of the Mercedes, she slammed the door, compressed her lips and balled her hands in her lap. Jake settled himself behind the wheel. They drove for miles without speaking. She longed to talk it all out, defuse some of the tension, but she couldn't find the words.

His gruff voice broke the silence. "That wasn't the first time I touched you." His gaze remained on the road. "It wasn't the first time you ran your hands through my hair."

Her heart lurched, and she pressed herself deeper into the soft leather seat. She wasn't ready to talk, after all.

Apparently he was. "Friday night we—"

"Can't we get past Friday night?" She pivoted in her seat to confront him. "It was a mistake, a misunderstanding. Let's leave it where it belongs—in the past."

"But it's not in the past."

She opened her mouth to argue, but honestly couldn't. Their sexual encounter wasn't in the past—at least, not for her. It had colored every moment since, both waking and dreaming, with hues and flavors of him. Of his lovemaking.

"I don't want to talk about what happened between us," she vehemently declared. "Not now, not ever."

He squared his jaw and kept his eyes on the road.

"And there's another thing I'm going to have to insist on," she said, "if I'm going to work with you."

"Such as?"

"No practical jokes. I won't tolerate them. And don't act like you don't know what I'm talking about." She barely noticed that they'd pulled off the highway and onto a shady graveled drive. "Since high school, you've done your best to make my life miserable for your own amusement."

He steered the car down the narrow drive and parked beneath a brilliant red maple. Pulling the keys from the ignition, he faced her, resting his arm along the back of the seats. "I'd say you're exaggerating a little, wouldn't you?"

"No, Jake, I wouldn't. You've danced me into swimming pools, sent a stripper to interrupt my speech at the civic club..." as she remembered, she grew angrier "...set off the smoke alarm at a hotel where I was staying. I had to run outside in the middle of the night!"

"Ah, yes. You were with your college debate team," he recalled, "visiting my campus." He barely suppressed a grin. "When I found out you were going to be there, I thought I'd welcome you."

"By videotaping me in my nightie?"

He furrowed his brow as if in deep concentration. "It was some pink ruffled thing, wasn't it? Came to about midthigh? And you had foam rubber tubes wound up in your hair."

"What happened to that videotape?" she demanded sharply, her anxiety renewed. "I worried for years that it would show up on a screen somewhere." *A Rowland Insurance business meeting, for example,* she thought, horrified at the prospect.

"No, no, that tape's for my own private collection." Mischief lurked again in his eyes.

"That's it!" She threw her hands in the air. "I can't work with you." Unbuckling her seat belt, she opened the car door.

"Brianna, wait."

Angrily she strode through crunching leaves and snapping twigs, beneath gold-leaf branches and past needle-sharp firs, her blood roaring in her head. One more minute with Jake would surely kill her! Unless she killed him first.

Heavy footsteps thudded and crackled; a strong hand

clamped around her arm. "Brianna!" He turned her to face him. "Do you really think I'd show that tape to anyone?"

"Anything for a laugh."

"Give me a little more credit. I'm beyond practical jokes. I swore 'em off years ago."

"It's high time you swear off your teasing, too."

His hands tightened on her arms, and his face darkened. "I could say the same to you."

"I don't tease you."

"You do, Brianna," he charged, his gaze harsh and unyielding. "You do."

The intensity of his stare diffused her thoughts into a visceral whirl—warming her, blaming her, scaring her. "When?" she asked in a bemused whisper.

"Right now. You have to know that all I want to do is take you to the nearest bed and finish what we started."

Her blood rushed. Her heartbeats shook her. "I told you not to talk about—"

"You can't get naked in a man's arms and do the things we did," he said forcefully, "then walk away and think he'll forget about it. He won't. *I* won't."

Her throat tightened. From his perspective, she had teased him. And she had no doubt that he wouldn't forget. She certainly wouldn't. Not ever. She'd wronged him. She *owed* him...

What was she thinking? Abruptly she pulled back from his grasp, struggling to reclaim her common sense. How, *how* did he always make right seem wrong and wrong seem so right? He was a danger to her, the worst kind of danger. She owed him nothing. What happened Friday night had been as much his fault as hers.

"There's a law against harassment of this kind," she

warned him, lashing out in self-defense. "You'd better learn it, now that you're my boss."

"If being your boss means I can't talk honestly with you, then I won't take the job."

Her lips parted. "But you can't quit!" Not for a moment did she doubt that he would. "The company is depending on you. So is the town. And Evan!"

He took a menacing step closer. "Then don't ask me to pretend I don't want you."

Warm reaction sizzled through her, and she had to remind herself that he wanted her body, not her. Sex. Just sex. But that distinction was rapidly dwindling in significance as his potent attraction kept growing stronger. She managed a choked whisper, "Take me home."

He stared darkly at her for another moment, then turned away. Expelling his breath in a long hard rush, he shoved his hands deep into his pockets and dropped his head back to stare up at the sky.

Confusion roiled in her as she watched him grapple with something she couldn't fathom. Sexual frustration, she guessed, but also the aggravation of having his will thwarted. She supposed very few people did that.

Slowly, cautiously his gaze lowered to hers. "Okay. If I have to treat you as a business associate, I will. If I can't mention the fact that we almost made love, that just holding you and kissing you almost made me come without ever getting inside you..." his voice dropped to a hoarse whisper "...which is where I want to be, Brianna." He paused and took a breath. "Then I won't mention it. But there will be times when I'm looking at you and I won't be thinking about work. No law or agreement between us is going to change that."

Drawing slowly away from her, he turned and stalked

back to the car. Brianna stayed where she was, afraid to move, afraid her legs might give way beneath her.

He threw open the trunk and grabbed a few bags. "Are you coming inside or not?"

"Inside?" The word suddenly sounded so sexual. She realized then that beyond the cluster of Douglas firs was a house. A rustic log cabin. "Where are we?"

"A hunting lodge." He slammed the trunk. "I rented it."

"You rented it?" Would he never stop surprising her? "For how long?"

"The day." His eyes met hers. "But we can get it for the night, too."

She shook her head in refusal, but a surprising wistfulness overtook her. What a way to spend the evening—alone with him in this picturesque little cabin, taking care of unfinished business— Abruptly bringing herself back to reality, she rehashed the reasons why she could never do that. A night or two in Jake's arms couldn't be worth permanently losing Evan. And because, for her, Jake had always been the devil incarnate: he spoiled her best-laid plans, lured her with temptation, made wrong seem right and generally tried to shove her down the road to ruin.

But she'd already been down that road. She'd lived there, thanks to the man who had played devil to her mother.

No, Evan was the kind of man Brianna needed, a man who couldn't lead her down the wrong path even if he tried. Which of course, Evan would never think of doing.

"So," she called out, squaring her shoulders with false bravado, "have you agreed to my terms?"

Jake halted near the cabin door, his arms loaded with photo albums and training manuals. "Your terms?"

"No practical jokes, no teasing, and we keep our relationship strictly business."

His lips closed in a straight, firm line. He looked annoyed.

She raised her brows, holding her ground. "Agreed?"

"I already told you I've sworn off jokes, and I'll try not to tease. As far as our relationship goes—" he paused, weighing his words "—we'll keep it any way you want it." He produced a key, unlocked the cabin and threw the door open.

Brianna supposed that would have to do for an agreement. What choice did she have, really?

As she contemplated her options—or lack thereof—he yelled from the doorway, "Break's over, Ms. Devon. I'm calling the meeting to order. Get your butt in here."

5

THE HANDS OF HIS watch were barely reading four o'clock when Brianna rose from her chair at the table cluttered with photo albums. "It's quitting time."

She insisted that he drive her home immediately. Quitting time. As if she had to punch a clock.

Jake knew he shouldn't let it bother him. She *had* spent the entire afternoon working. Despite the secluded intimacy of the cabin, their cozy lunch topped off with Amish apple pie, the blazing fire he'd built in the hearth and the neatly made bed in the corner—which she never ventured anywhere near—she'd focused entirely on his impersonation of Evan.

Business. All business.

Even so, Jake had found the afternoon surprisingly enjoyable. When she spoke about her co-workers she lost her cool restraint, her voice softened into gentle cheerfulness and her hazel eyes sparkled with droll humor. He'd seen and heard her this way a hundred times, but always from afar, always from the outside looking in. This time she spoke not to Evan or to her friends but to him.

He hadn't known how pleasurable being in the direct sunlight of her friendliness would be. He hadn't known how deeply she would penetrate him, how she would warm places inside of him.

Her announcement of quitting time had stunned him,

like ice water dashed over a sunbather. He felt almost as raw and shaken as he had the previous Friday night, when she'd stopped their lovemaking by calling him another man's name. He still felt the jolt from that. *And now, quitting time.*

What the hell did she see in Evan that was so lacking in him? More than ever, Jake wanted to know. Because the thought that he might never make love to her, might never taste her sweetness again, might never burn in her fire, had become intolerable.

He found himself grinding his teeth on their drive home.

THE MOMENT JAKE LEFT her at the curb of her house, Brianna headed for a cool shower to soothe the heat that had been radiating under her skin all day—sometimes from anger, but mostly from the unrelenting sexual power emanating from Jake. How she'd managed to distract herself and him with business, she'd never know. His husky words and bold stare so easily stoked her heat.

She whispered a thankful prayer that she'd have the weekend to prepare for their next confrontation. At least, she hoped she'd have the weekend.

Then, again...what would *he* be doing until Monday?

Curiosity took hold of her. Everywhere she went that Saturday and Sunday, she watched for him—in the grocery store, the bank, the church, knowing that his activities would reflect directly on Evan.

What if Jake was spending his time with a woman from town or from the office? Surely he wouldn't enter into a relationship pretending to be Evan...would he? Her anxiety level rose. She hoped that if Jake needed a woman, he'd at least fly out of town to find one.

Oddly enough, she found no comfort in that possibility.

In sore need of distraction, she joined Chloe for Sunday brunch at the Victorian inn she managed. On a private glassed-in porch where they sat with cappuccino, crescent rolls and mushroom-spinach quiche, Chloe asked, "So how's your relationship with Evan coming along?"

Brianna almost choked. She'd told Chloe the previous week that she hadn't gone through with her seduction after their makeover Friday night. She had not mentioned that Jake had been there, nor had she confided anything about the embezzlement and impersonation. Though she loved Chloe dearly and knew she could be trusted with most things, these secrets were too important to trust to anyone.

"I haven't seen much of Evan lately." And she hadn't thought about him much, either, she realized. Of course, she'd been so terribly distracted by Jake....

Chloe shook her tousled auburn locks. "I don't understand why you didn't go through with your plan Friday night. Are you sure you don't want to see a sex therapist?"

"I don't need a sex therapist!" *At least, not when I'm with Jake.* The thought hit her from out of nowhere. But it wasn't a fair deduction, was it? She'd gone that Friday night with seduction on her mind. If Evan had been there instead, she would have experienced the same slow burn of sexual desire...wouldn't she? Thoughts of Evan would now be tormenting her late at night... wouldn't they?

Chloe finished off the last of her quiche. "I think you need to let him know how you really feel. If you can't talk to him, put it in a letter."

Brianna froze with her coffee cup halfway to her mouth. She *had* written him a letter—and had tossed it into the interoffice mailbox, certain that Maude would forward it to him at his unknown address overseas. But Cy Rowland forbade any form of communication with Evan, which meant that her letter—her very personal letter about intimate problems—could end up in Jake's hands!

By the time she and Chloe had finished their brunch, the idea of Jake reading that letter had become too humiliating to contemplate. Praying that he hadn't read it yet, she decided to stop by the office and take it out of the mail pile—which she hoped to find on Maude's desk.

As she drove down a back street toward the office, a beige Mercedes passed her. Jake was behind the wheel. And beside him, in the passenger seat, was a redheaded woman.

Brianna stared through her rearview mirror as the Mercedes drove beyond her line of vision. Jake was with another woman. It didn't mean he was out on a date with her, Brianna told herself. They could be friends, or even relatives. But knowing Jake, that seemed highly unlikely.

She was stunned. Despite his reputation as a ladies' man, she hadn't really expected him to be with a woman. She felt hurt, as if he had betrayed her, although she had no claim on him whatsoever. She felt...she felt...terrible.

And it had nothing to do with the impersonation or the fact that Jake probably wasn't staying in character. It had everything to do with the thought of him holding and kissing another woman the way he'd held and kissed her.

AFTER PICKING UP the systems analyst from the Columbus airport—a tough old bird with cherry red hair, a penchant for cigarillos and an IQ of at least 200—Jake explained the nature of the computer problems. There'd been an attempted embezzlement, he'd told her, swearing her to confidentiality as he drove her to a hotel.

On his way home, his cellular phone rang, and he was relieved to hear Evan's voice cursing the French authorities, the embezzler who'd made an ass out of him and the idiots running the hotel where he was being kept. Only after he'd damned them all to hell did Jake pose his question.

"Are you ready to tell me what the hell's going on with the business?" The silence that followed made Jake's lips compress. "Talk to me, Ev. I just spent one hell of a weekend going over your books. The company's finances were pretty bad before the embezzlement ever took place."

"They're not as bad as they look," Evan argued. "This is just an awkward time for the company, that's all."

"An awkward time? Your cash reserve is so low you wouldn't be able to cover losses for even a quarter of the business on your books."

"A temporary problem because of a recent growth spurt."

"It's called spreading yourself too thin. You're in such a hurry to grow that you went after accounts too large for you to service. The premiums aren't enough to pay for the extra manpower, let alone cover the potential losses."

"Back off, Jake. Cy asked you to help us out of a tight spot, not dig your nose into my business."

"The old man doesn't know the risk you're taking, does he?" Again, a heavy telltale silence fell. "Why doesn't he know, Ev? He used to be on top of everything. How could he not know that you're close to losing your insurance license?"

"He hasn't been very involved in the last couple years," admitted Evan. "He gets confused. Tires too easily."

"Are you talking about the Cy *I* know?" Jake couldn't believe that his iron-willed grandfather could ever be anything less than a master of the game. Concern tightened like a band around his chest. "What's wrong with him?"

"He's just getting old. I've been taking on more and more responsibility. You didn't want any part of it, remember?" After another tense pause, he said, "Cy doesn't need to know every little problem that crops up."

"Every little problem?" A humorless laugh escaped Jake. "As long as you don't care about Rowland Insurance going under, I guess you can consider these problems 'little.'"

"Of course, I care! I've spent years building up the business. The decisions I made were in the best interest of the company. I'm counting on investments to supplement the reserve until we build up the premium base."

"Your investments are another matter. Why did you invest so much in speculative stock? You're breaking insurance regulations and taking a hell of a gamble."

"Don't preach to me. I was playing the stock market before you even knew that money was supposed to be made as well as spent. This is my company, Jake, and I don't want you messing with it."

"You might consider the company yours, but it belongs to the other stockholders as well."

"We didn't bring you in to analyze my effectiveness as CEO. Just play the part you were hired for."

"Okay. I'll just twiddle my thumbs in your office until you find a way out of the embezzlement charges. Meanwhile I'm sure Cy will be giving you a call about these deficits in your reserve and your high-risk investments."

"For God's sake, don't go worrying Cy. He'll have the whole board in an uproar. All I need is time."

"Either I implement the changes that have to be made or I turn the matter over to Cy. The choice is yours."

"You'll give him a heart attack, damn it! But you don't care, do you? As long as you're free to go and do whatever you please, why should you worry about the old man?"

"Which will it be, Ev? Cy or me?"

After a combustible pause, a blown out breath sounded across the wire. "Okay. You win. Go ahead and do whatever you can to increase the reserve. There won't be much you can do with the investments—they're too low to sell right now. But I'm sure they're on their way up. And, ah, Jake..." In a greatly humbled tone, Evan murmured, "Don't mention the problems to anyone else, either. Wouldn't want the employees in a panic."

"Nobody here will know."

"That includes Brianna, doesn't it?"

Jake's hand tightened again on the receiver. "Don't you think we can trust her with the truth?"

"I don't want her to know. She'd worry more than anybody. She thinks the employees are her little chicks and she's their mother hen."

"Afraid your halo might get tarnished, Ev?"

"Get off my back, Jake. I'm going through enough as it is." Evan's voice held a certain edge that told Jake he'd been pushed to his limit. An old protectiveness slid into place. Throughout their boyhood, the death of their parents and the endless parade of servants, they'd had only each other to count on. Jake's moral support of Evan had often made the difference between Evan handling a problem or caving in under its pressure. Jake knew he could deal with a lot more adversity than his brother could.

"They're trying to pin this embezzlement on me," Evan fretted. "I didn't have a damn thing to do with any of it."

"Calm down, Ev. We've got investigators combing the globe to find Cassandra Jones. And don't worry about what's going on here. I've pulled companies through worse problems than these. But I'm going to start making the necessary changes now, and I don't want any interference from you."

"Okay. It's in your hands until I get back. And, ah, mum's the word, right?"

Jake shut his eyes. That wouldn't be easy. "Right."

"Thanks, Jake."

"One more thing I need to know. What exactly is your relationship with Brianna?"

Another lengthy silence. Jake wasn't sure he could deal with this one. He wanted to reach through the wire and grab his twin by the throat.

"We were dating for a while, but I broke it off."

"That's it? You're not planning to kiss and make up?"

"Look, I'm already having to open my books to you. I don't see any reason to share details of my personal life."

"I'm living your personal life, damn it."

"All you need to know is that Brianna and I have

parted ways, except for our professional relationship."

"You're right there, bro. That's all I needed to know."

BY MORNING, BRIANNA decided she was glad that she had seen Jake with another woman, glad that she'd spent the night in torment. She considered it a wake-up call. Because somewhere along the way she'd begun to want him—in a purely physical way, of course. But wanting him in any way was crazy. Last night's agony had been proof of that.

Today she would ask Maude to return her letter, which she hadn't found the previous night, and then she would calmly, rationally discuss with Jake the ramifications of allowing anyone in town to know he wasn't Evan. If he should say that the redhead had believed him to be Evan, she would calmly, rationally point out how unfair his deception was.

She would not, under any circumstances, kill him.

Even before going to her own office, she took the elevator up to Evan's office suite on the top floor. Although it was an hour earlier than the usual starting time, Maude sat at her desk outside Evan's office. To Brianna's surprise, the glassed-in office behind her was also occupied.

Evan sat at his desk, talking on the phone! It had to be Evan. Jake would never come in this early. He wore an elegant dark suit and tie, immaculate white shirt, gold tiepin and cuff links that winked from French cuffs. He looked entirely at his ease, as if he wore such suits every day—it *had* to be Evan. How had he managed to come back so soon?

"Good morning, Ms. Devon," Maude said as Brianna stared in dazed surprise at the man behind the glass wall. "When did he...?" Her question trailed off when he leaned back in the chair and propped his legs up on his desk, lounging as if he were on the deck of a pleasure yacht.

No, indeed. Evan hadn't returned.

Her heart tripped into double time. The combination of Evan's elegant attire, Jake's virile nonchalance and the dark good looks shared by the brothers did something to her that restricted her breathing. He was, quite simply, magnificent.

As if mesmerized, she watched him hang up the phone and open a ledger, which he proceeded to study with apparent absorption. She wondered what was in the ledger. A girlie magazine? A racing form? A travel itinerary for his next volcano sprint? At least, he knew how to look busy.

"How long has he been here?" she asked Maude. He'd obviously left the redhead's bed early. Unless he hadn't been in the redhead's bed at all. Hope flickered madly in her heart. Disgusted with herself, she quelled it. What difference did it make to her whether he slept with the woman or not? She couldn't allow herself to care.

"I'm not sure when he arrived," Maude answered, her tone clearly indicating that no one, not even a co-conspirator, would get past her to violate Mr. Rowland's privacy, regardless of which Mr. Rowland he happened to be. "Shall I tell him you're here?"

Brianna suddenly felt unprepared to confront him. "No. If he asks for me, give me a buzz." She turned to leave. "Oh, and I think it might be wise for you to draw the blinds in his office."

They exchanged a look, and she knew Maude agreed that even though Jake looked exactly like Evan, he didn't behave the same way. Better to keep him safely out of sight from the employees. Questions and rumors about

"Evan's" odd behavior was the last thing they needed right now.

And the last thing Brianna herself needed was to stand there staring at Jake, spying on him, held in the grip of a fascination that bordered on being painful.

As Maude started for his office to draw the blinds, Brianna remembered the question that had brought her here so early. Striving for nonchalance, she inquired, "Have you sorted through Evan's mail from last week yet?"

Maude paused outside Jake's office door. "Of course. I put it on Mr. Rowland's desk."

A nervous lump settled in the pit of her stomach. Through the glass wall she saw that Jake had set up a computer beside the ledger he'd been studying. Maybe he hadn't actually read the mail, she thought with desperate hope. He'd probably been too busy playing video games on his notebook computer to bother with Evan's mail.

"I...I need my letter back. It was meant for—" She broke off, remembering that other co-workers could walk in and overhear. "The information in it is no longer valid. Would you please get it from his desk?"

"If he hasn't already opened it." Maude glanced at him through the glass wall. "He's on the phone again. I'll wait until he's off before I ask him for it."

The lump in Brianna's stomach turned over. Maybe he hadn't opened her letter because she'd marked it *confidential*. He might have realized how unethical it would be to read a confidential letter.

She winced at her own naïveté. This was Jake Rowland. Her letter would be the *first* one he'd open!

Realizing that she couldn't lurk outside his office while he talked on the phone, she made her getaway.

She wasn't ready to face him yet, especially not if he'd read her letter.

Less than ten minutes later, however, she *was* ready to face him. More than ready. After talking to a clerk near the coffeepot about maternity leave and a commercial underwriter in the elevator about the possibility of his early retirement, Brianna finally arrived at her own office for the first time that morning, only to find that her little paneled sanctuary had been invaded.

Her desk and her chair were missing! And she'd been stupid enough to believe Jake when he'd promised to behave!

She ran up the back stairway, too angry to speak to co-workers she might meet in the elevator. Breathless from the five-flight climb, she approached Maude's desk and demanded, "I need to talk to Mr. Rowland. *Now.*"

Maude looked up from her work in surprise. "Certainly, Ms. Devon. As a matter of fact, I was trying to buzz you—"

She didn't wait to hear more. Vaguely noting that the blinds had been drawn, she stormed into Jake's office, ready to tear into him for all of the aggravation he'd caused her—her missing desk, her miserable night, her waylaid letter.

He half sat at the edge of his desk—an odd place for him to be—and eyed her unannounced entrance with some surprise. "Ah, Ms. Devon. Come in."

"How can you think a stunt like that would be funny?" she blasted. "Hiding my desk is the most juvenile prank you've ever pulled. Didn't your promise to behave mean anything?"

He laughed—an oddly strained chuckle—and from his sideways glance, a suspicion crept up on her. Could it be that they weren't alone?

She turned to find a woman and two men sitting to the far left of his desk, all watching her with courteously muted interest. "Excuse me," she murmured, her embarrassment flaring. "I didn't realize—"

"Ms. Devon, I'd like you to meet the crew who will be working to solve our computer problems," Jake cut in smoothly. "This is Irene Cahn, one of the best systems analysts in the world. Irene, this is Brianna Devon, our human resources director."

Brianna received yet another jolt as she focused on the woman who had risen to shake her hand. From her short, smooth hairstyle and its vibrant color, Brianna recognized the redhead from Jake's car the previous day. Her deep voice as she greeted Brianna, her brusque handshake, her black suit and heavy flat shoes—all were undeniably masculine. She was also far older than Brianna had supposed.

Jake then introduced the two men as her associates, and Irene quipped in her gruff voice, "I'm just as surprised as you are to find us here, Ms. Devon. I'd like to know what kind of strings your boss pulled. I've never seen Ryan Alexander step in and take over a project of ours so we could start a new one that hadn't even been on our schedule."

Jake shrugged in response, offering no explanation.

"Ryan Alexander?" Brianna repeated. Jake's college buddy—the one who'd bet against him on his volcano run! "You're from Alexander Technologies?"

Irene nodded and the men broke into friendly small talk.

Another little light clicked on in Brianna's heart. Jake hadn't frivolously wasted time or raced across that volcano for bragging rights. He'd done it for them, for Rowland Insurance, to tackle their computer woes.

Irene lit up a slim cigar and explained the tactics they would use to track down the computer manipulations. Jake had apparently installed the team at a nearby hotel where they tied in by modem to the company's network. As Irene spoke, she addressed Jake as "Evan".

It didn't take a genius to realize the nature of Jake's relationship to her—purely business. Brianna's gladness bubbled up from deep within—a feeling she didn't want to analyze or even think about objectively. She just wanted to revel in the pure simple joy of knowing she'd been wrong about Jake. In more ways than one...

"I suggest we move this meeting next door," he said, nodding in the direction of Evan's sitting room. He ushered his guests in first, and then Brianna.

She stopped at the threshold and stared. Set among the plush armchairs, sofas and rosewood tables of the elegantly furnished sitting room were her executive desk and chair.

"This, by the way, is Ms. Devon's office." Jake avoided her stunned gaze as he addressed the others. "She can answer questions you have about personnel or whatever other information you'll need. Make yourselves comfortable."

As they settled into chairs and remarked about the view of the gardens from the window, Jake drew Brianna aside. "They know only about an attempted embezzlement. Ryan swears they'll be discreet. Help them as much as you can, then take them to lunch. Come see me afterward."

"But Jake," she said in a dazed whisper, "this office...it can't be mine. It's too...too..."

"Change it however you want." He dug in his pocket and handed her a key, presumably the one to unlock the outer door at the far end of the room.

"I don't mean that I don't like it. It's gorgeous. *Too* gorgeous. It should belong to a vice-president, at least."

An amused glint lit his deep blue eyes like sunshine on an ocean. "Okay. We'll change your title to vice-president of human resources."

"Don't you dare! Everyone would think I was sleeping with the boss."

He tilted his head, studied her intently. "Are you?"

"No! I mean...that's none of your business."

After a long, searching gaze, he uttered with finality, "The office is yours." He added in a deep, hoarse whisper, "I'll need you close at hand."

With a dizzying rush, she turned away, fighting an attraction almost too strong to hide. She didn't know this man. He wasn't the irresponsible boy she remembered or the hedonistic troublemaker she'd believed he'd become.

He was an enigmatic stranger who stirred her very blood with his presence. How would she ever keep her mind on business with an office that adjoined his? And why was she suddenly so very glad to be "close at hand"?

SOME TIME AFTER HE'D expected Brianna back from lunch, Jake waited on the phone for his call to be put through to his investment firm, absently shuffling through Evan's back mail. One letter caught his eye. There was no return address on the envelope except the initials B.D. It bore no stamp, so he knew it had come through the interoffice mail. And it was marked *confidential*. For Evan, of course.

With only a twinge of conscience, Jake drew the letter from its envelope. He would, after all, have to convey any important news the next time Evan called.

As Jake read, he slowly returned the telephone receiver to its cradle.

Dear Evan,
I understand why you think I regret our romantic involvement, but it isn't true. The problems we're having with physical intimacy are entirely my fault and have nothing to do with my feelings for you. I believe your patience and understanding are helping me to overcome my silly inhibitions. When you return, I hope to prove that to you. Yours always,

B.

The intercom buzzed. Jake ignored it as a maelstrom whirled within him. *She still wanted Evan.* He wasn't surprised; he'd carried around that knowledge heavy in his gut for a good long while now—in fact, since he'd met her. But reading it in her words, in her writing, jarred him as if he'd just now discovered it.

Forcing himself past the fact that she wanted his brother, he went on to analyze the letter further. What did she mean by "problems with physical intimacy"? For a bittersweet moment, a vengeful gladness touched him. If they had to be physically intimate—an idea that twisted his insides with something like pain—he was glad they were having problems. As much as he loved his brother, he simply could not want Brianna to find happiness in anyone's arms but his. He wanted her to be "physically intimate" in his arms, in his bed. There and only there.

Like a voice mocking him, he remembered her taunt after they'd almost made love. "I wasn't satisfied!" she'd yelled at him. "I was faking it!"

He hadn't believed her. He'd thought she was merely

reacting to his taunting of her. Could he have been wrong? As incredible as it seemed, the letter forced him to consider the possibility that all of that glorious passion had been one-sided. *No!* He'd felt the passion humming through her, heard it in her moans, tasted it like honey on her skin.

Had she been faking it? Every fiber in his being cried out that she hadn't. And yet, this letter clearly stated that she'd been having problems with physical intimacy.

With Evan, Jake silently specified.

His eyes fell on another passage from the letter, about overcoming her "silly inhibitions."

Not with Evan, he swore. On his life, he couldn't allow his brother to be the one to bring her to fulfillment...to show her the keen pleasure they could be sharing....

A brief knock sounded at his door, and Brianna herself peeked in. With his insides wrapped too tightly around themselves for him to speak, he gestured for her to enter.

"I'm back from lunch. Everything went well, I think." Her gold-green eyes regarded him with some new shyness that drew his attention like a bee to a blossom's nectar. "Just thought I'd tell you, though, that Evan would never sit on the edge of his desk like you were doing when I first walked in. He's not that—" She stopped midsentence.

Her gaze had lit on the envelope in front of him, then moved up to the letter he held. Her lips parted. Her face turned white.

She looked as if she'd gone into shock.

6

"YOU...YOU OPENED my letter," she breathed.

"Maude opened it. I didn't know it was yours," he lied. "There was no name or return address on the envelope."

"It was marked *confidential* and addressed to Evan."

"I have to open all his mail. What if the embezzler tries to contact him? Say, to cut some kind of a deal, or maybe even to try blackmail?" He saw the suggestion hit its mark. She hadn't considered that possibility. "If she would, we might be able to trace her."

"But her initials aren't B.D., which I wrote in the upper left corner of the envelope."

"You don't think she'd use her own initials, do you? She'd want to throw his guards off the track and get a letter straight through to him."

"It was interoffice mail!"

"She could have slipped in unnoticed to mail it." He ignored the scornful roll of her eyes. "Every piece of Evan's mail must be opened, and since I'm playing that role, I do the honors."

A charged silence settled between them.

"Have you...already read the letter?" she asked.

"Yes."

Her lips compressed. She inhaled deeply through nostrils that flared, raised her chin, and held out her hand. "Give it to me, please."

He handed the letter to her. With her face blazing, she crumpled up the page and stuffed it into the pocket of her tweed suit jacket.

"Brianna," he said gently, rising from his chair and starting toward her, "if you want to talk about what I read—"

"I don't." She turned away, running an unsteady hand over her braided twist, as if wayward tendrils had escaped. Visibly she struggled to pull herself together. "You stepped over the line in your impersonation this time," she said in a barely audible voice.

He'd stopped a short distance away from her, watching her profile. "Yeah, well that's where I'm having my problem...knowing when to be Evan and when to be Jake. Take, for instance, quitting time." He tried to keep the resentment out of his voice as he used her phrase from the other day. "Am I supposed to go back to being me? Stop in and visit old friends, buy rounds at Joe's Pub?"

"No, you can't. The whole town would know by morning. The impersonation would be a joke."

He moved closer, his gaze playing across her face. "If I have to be Evan on my off time, who am I supposed to call when I get lonesome? When I want...company?"

She stared at him. After silent reflection, she slowly replied, "I see what you mean. As long as people believe you're Evan, you can't engage in relationships—especially with women. It wouldn't be fair to Evan, or to the woman."

"Or to you, if the community considers you and Evan a couple. Does it?"

"Our close friends do and we've been seen together around town, but we've been very discreet. We haven't flaunted our romance. In fact, most of the employees at Rowland Insurance think we're just good friends."

"When in reality, you were much, much more than that."

Brianna stiffened. He was probing for information. Apparently he hadn't known from her letter that Evan and she had never made love. She wasn't about to tell him.

He frowned. A tiny muscle flexed in his jaw. "I won't play hermit the whole time I'm in town. Make up your mind, Brianna. Either I'm Evan or I'm not. Either we're a couple or we're not. And if we are," his gaze grew somehow intimate, "then come with me after work for supper."

"CHLOE, I KNOW YOUR Monday night football buffet attracts a crowd, but can you reserve a table for Evan and me this evening?"

"Of course."

"One close to the big-screen television, if possible."

"Your table will be waiting. How are things going with you two?"

"The same." She wished she could relieve some of the pressure building up inside of her by openly talking to Chloe, but she couldn't compromise the impersonation.

"Bri, you've got to loosen up with Evan if you don't want to lose him. He's a man, and men need—"

"Can't talk now, Chloe. Thanks for reserving us a table." Hanging up before Chloe could ask more questions, Brianna fell back in her chair with a sigh of relief. A table surrounded by shouting football fans seemed the perfect place to dine with Jake. They'd be out in public, yet everyone's attention would be on football instead of on "Evan" and Brianna.

Jake would have no way of knowing that she and Evan rarely went to restaurants during the week.

Usually on weekdays they ate at either her place or his, if he wasn't working on business projects or she on charity events. Supper at home with Evan had always been pleasant—a time to discuss the day's events, share viewpoints and generally unwind.

She didn't think supper alone with Jake at her place or his would lead to discussion at all. She certainly wouldn't unwind. She'd be worried about what might happen *after* dinner.

With Evan she had often snuggled up on the couch to watch television. Although he sometimes kissed her, trying to further their physical relationship, she'd always known she was in control. She'd felt safe knowing that this strong, powerful man wanted to please her, wanted to make her happy, even if it meant temporarily sacrificing his own pleasure. She'd longed to reward him for that—to make love to him, as he'd deserved.

She hated disappointing him. Yet, the situation was perfect for her. Evan played by her rules, advanced at her pace and behaved as she expected. His kisses never made her rational thought melt away; never made her want to forget tomorrow just to revel in the pleasure of the moment.

Jake's kisses had.

As much as she'd dreamt of being swept away to another dimension by a man's kiss, the reality of it terrified her. She'd seen what mindless attraction could do to a woman. She'd watched her stepfather emotionally abuse her mother, yet her mother always forgave. After every verbal onslaught, he would offer her a chance to appease him, taking her to their bedroom with her face still pale and wet with tears. It had sickened Brianna, although she'd been too young at the time to fully understand why.

By the time her mother's love for her second husband had burned out, she'd been stripped of all self-esteem, as well as the assets from her first marriage. She had no career, no home, no car, no credit cards in her name. She couldn't afford an attorney to fight against his powerful connections. She fled for sanity's sake, without a way to support herself or her eight-year-old daughter.

Brianna didn't want to think about her mother, who now felt safe in a new marriage, indentured to some new but kindly master.

And she didn't want to think about Jake's kisses. Mindless attraction was a dangerous thing, and she had to avoid it at all costs.

So why had she accepted his invitation to dinner? She should be angry with him for reading her letter. She didn't believe for one moment that he hadn't known it was from her. But she found herself unable to stay angry. *Good thing. You can keep an eye on him after work...for the sake of the impersonation.*

That was why she was glad he'd asked her to dinner, glad that he apparently intended to spend his off time with her. Her gladness had nothing to do with any mindless desire to be with him, to be close to him, maybe even in his arms....

"Give us a good table, Chloe," she whispered to herself, her eyes shut tight, her fist pressed to her forehead. "Right in the middle of the football crowd."

"THERE MUST BE some mistake." Brianna halted in the doorway of the private chamber to which the teenage hostess had led them. "I asked for a table near the television."

"Sorry, Ms. Devon, but this is the table reserved for you." The soft-spoken blond hostess, granddaughter of a co-worker, stood beside an elegant table set for two—the only table in the room. "The tables downstairs are all taken, in both the restaurant and the lounge."

"We're not very big on football anyway," Jake assured her from close behind Brianna. "This'll do fine."

"No, it won't," she insisted. The hostess had led them up a flight of stairs and unlocked the door to this cozy room with its piped-in music and flickering candlelight. Much too secluded. Much too romantic. "Amber, please get Chloe. Tell her—"

"Did you call, Bri?" Chloe appeared in the doorway, waving the hostess away and confronting Brianna with an innocent lift to her auburn brows. Dressed in a short black dress with diamonds sparkling at her ears, she was obviously ready for a date.

"This table isn't at all what I asked for," Brianna admonished. Chloe glanced past her toward Jake, and Brianna suddenly wondered if she would recognize him. Chloe had always been mildly infatuated with Jake. Evan, on the other hand, had never appealed to her on a personal level.

"Evan!" Chloe greeted enthusiastically, dodging Brianna's complaint. "Long time no see. How the hell have you been?"

"Super." He patted her briefly on the shoulder in a pseudopaternal kind of way, as if he were a minister or a well-respected community leader. "How about you, Chloe? All your ducks in a row?"

She responded with a droll anecdote about how busy the inn had been keeping her, and Brianna studied Jake in surprised approval. His reply was exactly what Evan's would have been—in content, tone and gesture—and she hadn't even coached him on it. She supposed she shouldn't be too surprised. They were, after all, twin brothers, born and raised together.

"Chloe," she cut in when the talk reached a lull, "I asked for a table near the television."

"Sorry. I did the best I could on such short notice. To make it up to you, I had the waiter ice down a bottle of my best chardonnay." She nodded toward a wine bucket beside the table. "And you won't have to go downstairs to the buffet. You'll be served a sampling of everything."

"But—"

"You'll have complete privacy so you can talk." She sent Brianna a meaningful look. Holding up a pager, Chloe instructed, "When you want service, just call with this."

"No, Chloe, we can't—"

"Sounds perfect." Jake took the pager with a smile so charming that Brianna felt sure Chloe would see through the impersonation immediately. "Chloe obviously went to a lot of trouble to make us happy," he said as Chloe studied him with new interest. "Let's not be ungrateful."

"Chloe, may I talk to you in private?" Brianna urged, mild panic setting in at the thought of spending time alone with Jake in this charming romantic room, which had probably once been a Victorian bedchamber.

"I don't have time, Bri. I'm already late for a date."

"Just out of curiosity, Chloe," said Jake, the devilish sparkle back in his eyes as he surveyed her sexy black dress with male appreciation, "where in Pleasantville are you going dressed like that?"

"*Not* the football buffet." With a wink and a measuring glance at him, she left them alone.

"But the game is an important one for my team!" Brianna called after her, feeling petty even as she said it.

Slipping an arm around her shoulders as if to comfort her, Jake swept her toward the table. "Which team is that?"

She caught her bottom lip between her teeth. She had no idea which teams were playing tonight. "Miami."

"You're in luck." He pulled out a chair for her at the round candlelit table. "Miami's not playing until Sunday." With hands firm and warm at her shoulders, he guided her down into the chair. "Besides, you hate football, remember?"

She salvaged some of her dignity by arranging her slim tweed skirt around her knees and settling gracefully into her seat. Evan never would have maneuvered her to a table against her liking. He never would have overruled her preference in favor of his own. She should be missing him dreadfully. She really should.

"You used to say football was too violent," Jake reminded her.

"I'm trying to appreciate the subtleties of the sport."

"Broadening your horizons. I like that." He settled into the other chair, his eyes warm with humor. "We'll have to catch the Miami game Sunday. I'm not sure if it'll be broadcast here, but I have a satellite dish that should pick it up." In a deliberately provocative tone, he added, "At, uh, my place."

She suppressed a traitorous upturn of her lips. He obviously knew she didn't want to be closeted in this private room with him or committed to spending an evening at his place. Planting her elbows insolently on the table, she rested her chin on her interlocked fingers and raised a brow. "Did I say Miami? I meant Ohio State."

"Ah, so you're into *college* football." Devils danced in

his deep blue eyes, thoroughly captivating her. "Maybe I can help you in your quest to appreciate the game. Show you a few moves from my quarterback days."

An involuntary laugh escaped her. "No thanks. I remember your tackle all too well."

Silence followed her lighthearted quip. Surprise had entered his gaze. She realized she'd broached a subject they hadn't discussed in the entire ten years since he'd tackled her behind the bleachers and doused her with salt water—a subject she'd never intended to mention. The same subject had sent her running from the conference room less than a week ago. She did indeed remember his tackle.

"And I remember your defensive moves," he said, his voice soft, his gaze unexpectedly sober. She sensed no teasing spirit in him now, no mockery. "Just to give you fair warning, ma'am—I'm still going for that touchdown." His sensuality warmed her like potent brandy. "In fact, I intend to win the game."

She strove to resist the heady effect of his gaze and words. "That's something you've never understood. I'm not playing a game."

"You're not? Then talk to me openly, Brianna. Let's say what's on our minds."

She frowned, trying to mask her alarm. She couldn't possibly tell him what was on her mind, what had been on her mind since he'd carried her to his bed. "Regarding what?"

"Us."

"There is no 'us,' unless you mean Evan and me."

"No, I mean Jake and you. But if you can't bring yourself to tackle that subject, let's start with your sudden need to watch football."

The beginning of a smile softened her mouth, and Jake

felt an immediate tug of response. She was just so damn beautiful. He wanted her with a need that made him ache. "You're afraid to be alone with me."

Their eyes locked and the same tension that had sparked years ago arched between them. He sensed a slow shift taking place somewhere within her.

"Maybe I *am* afraid." Her voice had gone all soft and throaty, reminding him of when he'd had her beneath him in bed, her silken hair free from its upsweep and glimmering across his pillows, her body his for the taking.

"Why?" he demanded, his own voice too hoarse and hard. "I'd never force you into anything, Brianna. I think I proved that the night you called me Evan. I stopped before you even knew you wanted me to."

Color warmed her face. "I know you'd never force me."

"Then why are you afraid to be alone with me?"

"Because you confuse me," she whispered, her eyes luminous with accusation. "You twist things around, Jake! Make right seem wrong and wrong seem right."

"Like making love?"

"Yes."

"You think it's wrong?"

"With you."

Her reply set his heart on edge, precariously balancing above a dark precipice. He grasped at a straw of hope. "But I make it seem right?"

She looked away from him, fixed her gaze on the swaying candle flame.

He had to restrain himself from taking her face in his hands and forcing her to maintain their connection. He wanted to know her answer. *Needed* to know it.

"Brianna." He clenched his teeth in frustration. "Damn it, *you don't belong to Evan.*"

That seemed to hit a nerve. Her gaze jerked back up to his. "I know that better than anyone. I don't *belong* to any man, and I never will."

He regarded her in surprise. He hadn't expected such a vehement reaction. He wanted to know what had generated it, wanted to peek through the sudden crack in her armor.

"I belong to myself," she swore with quiet passion. "Even if I marry someday, I'll still belong only to myself. When I'm faithful to a man, it's not because he owns me or because I owe him my loyalty. It's only because I don't want anyone else." Golden green fire flashed from her eyes.

"If you belong to yourself, Brianna," he replied, leaning forward to gaze even deeper into those eyes, maybe deep enough to see through the flames, "then be faithful to yourself when you answer this question."

Her attention centered fully on him. He had no doubt that she'd strive to answer with absolute honesty, even if she didn't answer aloud.

"Do you want only Evan?"

She went perfectly still—a stillness so profound he felt it in his bones. His chest tightened as he envisioned her leaving the table—the ultimate answer to his question.

But she didn't rise. She didn't seem to even breathe. "If you mean physically," she finally whispered, her eyes wide, her vulnerability clearly evident, "then I suppose I'd have to answer 'no.'"

A groundswell of emotion rose in Jake, robbing him of his voice, of his breath. Did she mean she wanted *him*, or was he jumping to the conclusion he hoped for?

Their stares intensified; each heartbeat peeled away another layer of the barrier between them.

A knock sounded at the door, disrupting the odd moment, startling Brianna into a realization of what she'd admitted. Evan wasn't the only man she physically desired. In fact, she wasn't sure she physically desired Evan at all, no matter how much she wanted to.

A waiter entered with a tray and set steaming aromatic plates of Amish-style Swiss steak, potatoes, vegetables and rolls in front of them. Brianna busied herself by opening her napkin on her lap. She smiled politely at the slender waiter as he uncorked their bottle of wine and poured them each a glass. All the while, her thoughts chased themselves in a dizzying whirl around her heart.

Why should she physically desire one man when she logically wanted another? It wasn't fair. It wasn't wise. It wasn't in her blueprint for her future. And admitting her weakness to Jake had been the pinnacle of foolishness. The tension between them had been strong enough since he'd read her personal letter. He shouldn't know these sexual secrets of hers, shouldn't have such inside knowledge.

And yet, he did.

The moment the waiter left them alone with only the background music to break the silence, Jake interrupted her first taste of supper with a quiet, yet fierce question. "If you're saying what I hope you are—that you want me the way I want you—then what's stopping us?"

She washed a bite of steak down with the dry, fragrant wine and barely escaped choking. As she touched her lips with her linen napkin, she reflected that choking might have been better than surrendering herself once again to his seductive stare. "The only reason I ever thought of you in that way at all," she said, her voice weak and tremulous as she reasoned through this madness, "is because of what happened between us that night. It was wrong. A mistake."

"The only mistake I made was stopping too soon." ·

She stared at him, struggling against a realization. She, too, wished he hadn't stopped. What was happening to her? In a bemused whisper, she asked, "Is that why we can't forget? Because we...didn't finish?"

He looked oddly hesitant to accept that explanation. "I guess there's only one way to find out." He leaned forward. "We've got to finish."

He was doing it again, she realized—making wrong seem so right. Decisively she shook her head.

"Why not, Brianna?" he probed with a quiet fierceness. When she offered no explanation, his jaw hardened. "Does it have to do with the problem you mentioned in your letter?"

"Of course not!" she cried, mortified. "My personal problems with Evan have nothing whatsoever to do with—"

"Are you sure those inhibitions you wrote about aren't keeping you from my bed?"

She lapsed into a stunned silence. Relentlessly he searched her eyes for an answer. She didn't want to give him one; at least, not the true one. The inhibitions that kept her from making love to Evan hadn't come into play at all with him. Quite the opposite. Even rightful inhibitions dissolved all too easily when Jake touched her.

Why, then, had the mere thought of him ruined her intimacy with Evan?

"I can help you, Brianna." The earnestness in his gaze left her no doubt of his sincerity. "Whatever kind of problem you're having, I swear I'll help you overcome it."

The irony wasn't lost on her. Here he was, offering to help her overcome her problem, when *he* was her problem!

It was then that the answer became obvious. He *could* help overcome it. He was probably the only one who would ever be able to help her.

When a person falls off a horse, how does conventional wisdom say to overcome a fear of horses? To climb back up into the saddle. When a person is afraid of water, he needs to swim. When a person is afraid of the dark, he needs to learn how to appreciate that darkness.

Why wouldn't the same kind of confrontational therapy work for her? Some deep emotional conflict must have formed in her adolescence because of her repressed sexual attraction to Jake. She obviously needed to resolve that conflict before she could move on to a truly fulfilling relationship. She needed to confront the problem by making love to Jake! Prove to herself that nothing traumatic would come of it.

As he'd pointed out, she didn't belong to Evan. Evan had broken up with her. Their relationship was over. Strangely enough, she felt no pain or anguish; only a sense of loss.

She had to move on. She owed it to herself now to overcome whatever mental block she'd developed because of Jake—the one that had led to her breakup with Evan.

"Brianna?" He watched her with concern. "Are you okay?"

"Yes. Yes, I'm fine." More than fine, she realized. Nervous though she was, she felt surprisingly free.

"I'm not trying to upset you or make you uncomfortable," he swore. "You're helping me and my family with this impersonation. I think it's only fair that I help you."

Shyness weighted her tongue. She struggled against it, forcing herself to speak words that came out agonizingly slow and halting. "Thank you, Jake, for your offer. I'd be very grateful for any...help...that you could give me."

At first she thought he hadn't quite understood what she was telling him. He moved not a muscle, blinked not an eye. The only response she detected was a subtle flush that illuminated his tan. He reached for his wine and took a drink of it, his dark blue eyes never leaving her face. When he set down his glass, he murmured, "You understand that I'm talking about helping you overcome your sexual inhibitions."

Without breaking their stare, she nodded.

Jake felt his soul rise up from his body and hover someplace above it. He saw his hand clench around the wineglass, sensed the slow intake of breath that seemed necessary to cool the throbbing in his skin. She was saying she'd make love to him.

The enormity of that fact filled him with an almost spiritual awe. He'd waited so long, he'd wanted her so badly. He hardly dared to believe she'd be in his arms, in his bed.

"We'd have to be discreet." Her shy, trembling voice somehow helped him believe she meant to go through with it. "Our business would have to stay our own. You'd have to promise me that."

"I promise."

"Our personal relationship couldn't interfere in any way with my career. I'd need your word on that, too."

"You have it."

She dropped her gaze from his and reached for her

fork, as if his promises had sealed the deal to her satisfaction, freeing her to carry on with supper as usual. But once the fork was in her hand, poised convincingly over her plate, she seemed to forget how to proceed from there.

He didn't bother to pick up his own fork. The hunger growing in him had nothing to do with food. He wanted to touch her, to hold her.

He reached across the table and intercepted her hand as it hovered aimlessly above her plate. Her surprised gaze met his. He took the fork from her, set it aside and drew her hand into his own. "Let's dance."

"Dance! Here?"

"Yes, here."

She glanced around. "There's no dance floor."

He stood up and pulled her with him. "If I'm going to help you," he whispered as he brought her into his arms, "you have to trust my lead." She didn't argue, but he felt her hesitation. He ran his hand up her back, beneath her stiff suit jacket, and molded her soft, warm body to his. Pleasure coursed through him in a current so strong he had to close his eyes to contain it. With his lips against her ear, he managed to say, "Promise to trust my lead?"

"I promise." Gradually she yielded, moving with him to the slow, subtle gyrations of the love song.

"I'm not just talking about dancing," he whispered.

"I know."

He pressed his chin against her temple and swept her into a turn, thoroughly intoxicated by her. The fragrance of her hair, the feel of her skin through body-warmed silk, the knowledge that he'd be making love to her soon, crested over him like waves breaking against a shore, each one lifting him higher.

Tonight. He'd take her home tonight.

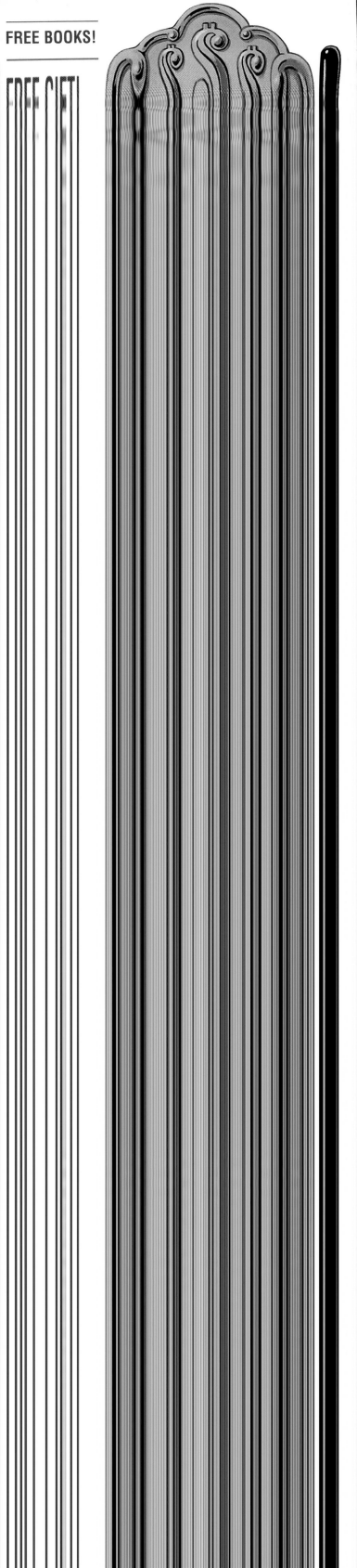

It seemed too good to be true. Was it? Was she acting on impulse? Would she come to her senses and stop, or even worse, blame him afterward? No! This time was different. She knew exactly who he was and she'd asked for his help.

His help.

He tightened his hold on her. He knew how to help her, didn't he? He knew how to kiss her—God yes, he remembered their kisses—and how to make her shiver and cry out loud.

But she'd said she'd been faking it.

Apprehension invaded his euphoria. She'd been lying, he knew. And even if on some slim chance she hadn't been, that didn't mean he couldn't make her happy now. The inhibitions she'd mentioned in her letter wouldn't stop him from pleasing her, couldn't possibly stop him from pleasing her.

Could they?

The song ended and he slowed their movements to a standstill but kept his arms around her, unwilling to let go. Whatever the problems were, they had to be serious, or she'd never have turned to him for help. Only an egotistical fool would discount the possibility that his desire and expertise in the art of lovemaking might not be enough.

The music changed to a faster tempo. He didn't move or free her from his embrace. She pulled back enough to gaze up at him, her eyes wide and golden and dazed with the same drugging sensuality he'd felt only moments before.

And he knew. Beyond a doubt, he knew. He'd find a way to reach her, to fan those sexual embers that smoldered so beautifully within her, until every inhibition she'd ever had burned away in the flames.

But he'd have to go slow. Take his time. Let her desire build beyond any she'd ever known. A dozen ways immediately leapt to his mind. He could redefine the term "teasing" for her, by God....

But could he himself stand it, when just the thought of waiting was making him crazy; when he wanted her so badly right now?

In a whisper low and rusty, he asked, "Do you want to finish dinner?"

"I don't think so."

"Let's go."

He paid the bill, helped her into her coat and ushered her out of the restaurant, into the frosty October night air, where their breath clouded and tiny snowflakes danced. Hurrying to his car, he huddled her against him, marveling at his freedom to do so, marveling at how much he wanted to kiss her.

As he opened the car door for her, their eyes met. Tension crackled like lightning between them. The ten-minute drive to her house took forever. Neither of them said a word. With each passing mile, the need in him intensified.

He could spend the night loving her. The knowledge burned within him. *But look at the bigger picture,* an inner voice warned. *She needs your help. Take things slow. If you move too quickly, you may never get another chance.*

And one night of her would never be enough.

He parked the car in the driveway of her snowy-roofed bungalow and escorted her up the walkway. She searched her purse until she found her keys. He took them from her and opened the door.

In the lilting shadows of the porch, she turned her face up to his. Hesitantly she whispered, "Do you want...?"

It was all the invitation he needed. Bracing her face in

his hands, he kissed her—deep and slow and with all the chaotic longing inside of him. He could allow himself this much tonight—a kiss, only a kiss, to kick start her desire. But when she wrapped her arms around his neck and gave herself over to him with sweet, thorough abandon, desire ripped through him like wildfire.

"Yes," he whispered between hot, intricate kisses, shouldering the door further open, "I want."

7

THEY STUMBLED SIDEWAYS into the entry foyer, their kisses evolving into voluptuous full-bodied explorations. The pleasure, the sweetness, grew sharp and intense, and the only thought left in Jake was to love her.

Without disrupting their kisses, he unbuttoned her coat, her blouse, her skirt, pushing and tugging them off her. She fumbled with his jacket, his shirt, his zipper. Clothing hit the floor in a direct path to the bedroom.

He claimed each new exposure of her with greedy, questing hands. When her curvaceous warmth became too much to savor with his hands alone, he broke away from their erotic tongue play to lave her breasts—tiny tastes, then succulent swirls, until he'd filled his mouth with her.

A soft groan, a cry. Her fingers in his hair...

Urgency overtook him. He swept her onto the bed and yanked the last barrier of white lace down her legs. Long legs. Velvet skin. *Beautiful, beautiful...* Fire in her gaze, igniting his blood.

Brianna...his. He loved her in earnest, as he'd dreamt of for so long, thrusting himself deep within her. Her vibrant heat closed around him with an awesome tightness, a virtual suction. Sublime pleasure. He wanted to prolong it, to share it, but he couldn't hold back. His passion surged out of his control, raging and bucking, then exploded into a rapture that stunned him.

He couldn't move. Couldn't breathe. Held her tightly, his insides quaking.

It wasn't until later, much later, as she lay with her face against his shoulder, that rational thought filtered through to his brain.

And he realized he'd been an animal. Worse than an animal, because he'd known better. He'd torn off her clothes, thrown her across the bed and taken her in a savage rush.

"Brianna?" he breathed, brushing a hand that still trembled over her silky, fragrant hair. "Are you okay?"

She nodded. With her cheek pressed against his shoulder, she was obviously hiding, refusing to lift her head and meet his gaze.

Self-recriminations flooded him. He was supposed to be helping her. If any of her inhibitions had cropped up along the way, he certainly hadn't noticed. His attention had been focused entirely on his own driving need.

But even as he mentally cursed his caveman behavior, awareness of her invaded his senses. She lay naked in bed with him, the woman he'd fought so long to have, her lush, slender body still hot and moist from loving. If she moved her hip to the right, she'd know how much of an animal he really was.

Because he wanted her again.

"I'm sorry if I was...uh...rough, or too rushed," he uttered. "I don't know what came over me. I don't usually...I mean, that wasn't the way I—" He stopped, unable to explain, even to himself, how desperately he'd wanted her.

A lame excuse for forgetting the reason she'd brought him to her bed—to help her overcome inhibitions. What if he'd made them worse? What if he'd scared the hell out of her, taking away any chance for her to fully enjoy sex? He had to know. He had to set things right, at any cost.

"Brianna!" He shifted around to look into her face, forcing her to lift her head. "Did I do anything that you didn't like, anything that upset you?"

At first he thought she wouldn't answer, her hazel gaze unreadable in her flushed heart-shaped face. But after a moment, she replied in a voice hushed and throaty, "If you did, it happened so quickly I didn't have time to notice."

He saw it, then—a glimmer in her eyes, a slight curl to her lips. Could she be *teasing* him?

"I'd heard you like fast women." She stretched out beside him, her head propped up on one arm as her hair cascaded in shining waves. "Now I know why. A woman's got to be quick with you or she'd miss the action altogether."

When he came to grips with his astonishment, he squared his jaw, acknowledged her wit with a grudging half smile and grabbed her.

Merciless in his vengeance, he made her cry out in surprise, then shriek in laughter, as she fought to disengage his fingertips from the ticklish valleys between her ribs.

"So you think I'm fast." He dragged her to him and trapped her body beneath his, thoroughly relishing their skin-to-skin skirmish. "Want a slo-mo replay?"

"Stop! No more t-tickling," she begged, panting from laughter and the exertion of the fight...and then maybe from the sensation of his chest rubbing across her nipples, sharpening them into diamondlike peaks.

Obligingly he moved his fingers from her rib cage, letting them wander to other sensitive places. He rained kisses across her breasts, then tugged at a nipple with his mouth. Her struggles turned to writhing, her laughter to moans. Desire picked up force, like a steam locomotive, until his insides burned with sensual hunger. He was man, she was woman, and he wanted to mate with her again, like the animal he was.

He wanted her hot and wild this time. He coaxed her there with his tongue and his fingers until sobs sounded deep in her throat. Bracing his knees on the mattress, he captured her hips and penetrated with slow and shallow undulations, pushing ever deeper. She wrapped her legs around him and arched into his thrusts. The bed creaked and groaned. The headboard banged harder and harder against the wall. His rhythm quickened until the savagery surpassed even that of their first coupling.

He climaxed along with her, their cries intermingling, then rode out the pangs of pleasure.

Their energy spent, they collapsed into a tangle of limbs and bedsheets, an intimate cocoon, where they drifted off into exhausted slumber. Even as he slept, Jake knew he held Brianna, and pleasure radiated through him.

He awoke at five in the morning. She dozed soundly beside him, her lashes thick and curved against her face. An odd feeling of awe overcame him, as if he were experiencing something cosmic.

Something cosmic.

With a little quirk of fear, he tore his gaze away from her and forced himself out of her bed. He had to get his thoughts together, put this whole thing into perspective. *Keep it light.* Everyday life had to go on. He had to get home to shower, shave and dress for work. *Keep it light.*

Impatiently he searched for his clothes among the ones they'd strewn on the floor. When he found them, he dressed with quick, silent tugs in the early morning darkness.

Nothing extraordinary had happened. Why should he feel that it had? He'd made love to a woman—a beautiful, desirable woman whom he'd wanted for a long time, yes—but lovemaking wasn't some mystical happening. The sex had been good; he'd admit that much. Better than any he'd had in a long time. Better than he'd believed possible...

Keep it light.

Had he given her what she'd wanted? He tried to remember any signs she might have shown of being inhibited. She hadn't hidden herself in shyness or stopped him. In fact, he'd never had a warmer, more responsive partner, or one who'd aroused him to the same incredible heights.

Would she want him again? His life wouldn't end if she didn't. His heart wouldn't stop pumping or turn to stone. *Keep it light.*

Dressed in yesterday's clothes, he scribbled a brief note: "Had to go. Didn't want to wake you. See you at the office. J." Then he strode out of her house without risking another look at her.

If he hadn't pleased her, he would take it in stride. But not now. Not until he'd put it all into perspective.

"HURRY, BRIANNA, WE'RE late for a meeting."

Theresa, her stout dark-haired secretary, held the elevator doors open as Brianna dashed through the front lobby, shrugging out of her coat on the way. She'd never overslept before. She'd never been late. Why today, of all days? She knew why, actually. Because no man had ever drained her so completely of energy or transported her to another galaxy, as Jake had the previous night.

Then, he'd left her without a kiss or a goodbye. Only a note on her bedside table. Why?

"Mr. Rowland buzzed me and asked where you were," said Theresa, her brown eyes wide with concern as she ushered Brianna into the elevator. "I was worried about you."

"I'm just running a little late." Brianna draped her coat over her arm and tried to collect herself. As the floor numbers flashed at the top of the elevator, her nervousness grew. She'd be facing him soon, the man who had made love to her so thoroughly, then left before she awoke.

Why was she feeling so anxious about seeing him? Just because they'd had a night of incredible sex didn't mean she'd fall under some dark spell of his. True, he had worked powerful magic on her last night. She'd never imagined, never dreamed that such passion existed, or that her body could so completely rule her. But why should she feel threatened by that? She'd never let sex get in the way of important things.

"Thanks for waiting, Theresa," she murmured as they reached the third floor, where meetings were held. "I wasn't aware we were having a meeting this morning. Who called it?"

"Mr. Rowland."

"Mr. Rowland! Are you sure?"

"Yes, ma'am. It surprised everyone."

It certainly surprised Brianna. Why on earth would he call a meeting? Did he even know how to conduct one?

"You don't mean Mr. Cy Rowland, do you?"

"No, our very own Mr. Evan Rowland," Theresa said with a grin. "He's been doing some unexpected things lately."

Brianna's heart took a leap. Had their impersonation

been blown? She searched the friendly face of her matronly secretary for any signs of suspicion. "What do you mean?"

Theresa shrugged. "He moved your office upstairs without any notice. I know you said he'd been planning that for a while, but no one mentioned it to me."

"I'm sorry. That was an oversight on my part. Your desk and filing cabinets should be moved sometime this week to the office outside mine. It's much more private up there. You'll like it."

"Of course I'll like an office in the penthouse. Who wouldn't?" She flashed her usual good-natured smile, but soon a reflective look took its place. "Mr. Rowland *has* been acting strange, though. Yesterday, Millie in auto claims said he asked how her son is doing in football."

"What's strange about that? Her son began varsity football last month, didn't he?" Brianna had mentioned that fact to Jake as they'd pored over photos of the employees.

"Sure, but Mr. Rowland has never spoken a word to Millie before. She didn't think he even knew her name, let alone that she has a son in high school. And do you know what Mr. Rowland said to me when he was looking for you this morning?"

Foreboding gathered in her stomach. "What?"

"He said, 'Good morning, how are you,' in Italian."

"So?"

"How does he know I speak Italian?"

"Your last name *is* Rosetti."

"Pat's last name is DeLuca, and she doesn't know a word of Italian. Tony's name is Gianelli, and he wouldn't know the difference between Italian and Chinese."

Brianna scolded herself for telling Jake too much. She'd mentioned that Theresa had moved to the United States from Italy when she was a child. After forty-some years in Chicago, her English held no trace of an accent. Brianna realized now that Evan himself probably *didn't* know anything about Theresa's background. He hadn't hired her; Brianna had, the previous year, when Theresa moved to Pleasantville.

With some surprise, Brianna reflected that Evan and she had never talked about employees without a reason to do so. The need to discuss the clerical staff simply hadn't come up.

"I think I mentioned to Mr. Rowland that you speak Italian," she explained as they exited the elevator.

"He speaks it very well." She frowned in puzzlement. "That was the first time he's said anything more to me than absolutely necessary. He's much friendlier than I thought."

They lapsed into silence as they reached the meeting room. Embarrassed for being late, Brianna's first impulse was to sit in a seat at the back. But apprehension about mistakes Jake might make forced her to a seat near the front, where he would see her if he needed help.

A tingling awareness rushed through her as she heard the deep, familiar baritone of the man at the front of the room—dramatically handsome with his athletic physique, burnished hair, deep tan and vivid blue eyes that hadn't acknowledged her entrance with even the briefest of glances. His expensive suit jacket had been tossed across the unused podium and his crisp white shirtsleeves were rolled up over muscled forearms. He spoke with an easy nonchalance—vastly different from Evan's formal style. Yet no one would mistake him for anything less than the man in charge. Like his grandfather, he radiated power and control.

He was talking now about sales made in personal and commercial lines. "Our sales force deserves a lot of credit. They've been extremely productive this year." He named the top sales managers and reps. Brianna was surprised he knew the statistics. The sales leaders stood and accepted the obligatory round of applause. Brianna could almost hear the teeth gritting from much of the audience. The sales department had been putting a lot of pressure lately on underwriting, actuarial and claims, to help get and keep large accounts. Tempers had been flaring all across the board.

"Our other leaders deserve recognition, too," Jake said, again surprising her as he called names of key employees in every department. Brianna realized he'd gleaned those names from her, when he'd asked whom she considered the unsung heroes. She remembered being surprised by the question as they'd browsed through photos.

"These are the folks who keep us stable," declared Jake. Applause, cheers and whistles for these hardworking employees shook the room. "I'll be calling each of you individually to my office today," Jake told them. "I'd say it's time to open our lines of communication, wouldn't you?"

Wild applause answered his question.

He went on to announce an "idea drive." Anyone with suggestions, complaints or comments should put them in a box that would be installed in the break room. He promised to read each one. Employees whose ideas resulted in a change would be rewarded with their choice of money or time off. "If you prefer to remain anonymous, that's fine, too."

More applause thundered. If Brianna hadn't known of the impersonation, she would have been as hopeful as everyone else that a change in policy might be underfoot, giving more support and recognition to the "naysayers," the ones who dared turn down new business for the sake of stability. She did know better, though. Evan had felt a need to grow, and she trusted his judgment implicitly—although the engineers and underwriters who argued against the larger accounts had made a good case, too.

Jake was obviously just grandstanding. Concern curled through Brianna. She hated to see the employees' hopes raised, then left unfulfilled. Funny, though, how Jake had zeroed in on the problem that had been dividing the workforce.

He chatted and joked for a few minutes more. By the time the meeting adjourned, the mood was jovial and upbeat.

"See what I mean?" whispered Theresa. "What'd he do, take a 'friendly' pill or something?"

Brianna saw exactly what she meant. It was the same as it had been in high school—Jake winning scores of friends with easy camaraderie, Evan earning respect with hard work. She'd have to keep Jake out of the limelight before too many people noticed the difference.

As managers and executives approached him with questions, Brianna took Theresa to her new office and went over paperwork and reports. As they finished their discussion, her intercom buzzed. "Ms. Devon?"

It was Jake. Still feeling inexplicably intimidated at the prospect of talking to him after last night's intimacy, she pressed her intercom button and replied with a curt, "Yes?"

"Will you step in here for a moment, please?"

"Certainly." With a few parting instructions for Theresa, she headed to Jake's office. Ideas flitted through her mind on how she'd approach him, what she'd say and do. None seemed right.

She stepped through their adjoining doorway to find him seated at his desk and Maude beside him with a notepad, busily writing. Brianna realized then that she'd never be able to look at him the way she once had. He was no longer a dangerously attractive adversary. She'd known his body, his passion, his way of turning a woman inside out. He'd been deep inside her, spilled his seed into her. She knew him in the biblical sense, and she was stunned at how deep a bond she suddenly felt with him.

It could come to no good. It frightened her.

He noticed her in the doorway. "You were late."

"I overslept."

He tilted his head, meeting her gaze with the impersonal detachment of a boss in casual conversation with a subordinate. "Up too late last night, Ms. Devon?"

As if he didn't know damned good and well. "Very."

"No problems, I hope." The slight softening of his voice would be taken by anyone listening as courteous concern.

"No." She averted her eyes as warmth crept into her face. *Why did you leave without saying goodbye?* "No problems."

"Good." Silence went on a moment too long, and she glanced back up at him. His gaze embraced her with the intimacy of a secret kiss. "Glad to hear it."

Her body responded with a hot surge. She couldn't let herself be drawn into a sensual haze by a mere look from him, or by references to their night together. Lifting her chin, she reclaimed her poise and saw with relief that

Maude had been occupied with her note taking. "I must say, Mr. Rowland, that the meeting you held was quite a surprise. You certainly know how to put on a good show."

"That's how you saw it...a good show?"

"What more could it possibly be?" When he didn't reply, she added, "I hope others didn't take it as anything more."

"I hope they took it for what it was—a talk from their CEO." Though his tone had remained pleasant, he had effectively reminded her that he did, in fact, hold that position. "Now, Ms. Devon, I'd like you to pull the personnel files of the people I'll be meeting with today. Maude will give you the list when she's transcribed it."

Smarting from his subtle reprimand and surprised by his request, Brianna briefly nodded.

He went on. "I'll also need you here to fill me in on anything I should know about each supervisor and his department."

"I have a few prior commitments, but I suppose I can postpone most of them."

"Please do." He glanced at his watch, picked up the phone and dismissed Brianna with a nod. Maude handed her a list of employees whose files were to be pulled. Bewildered by Jake's plans, Brianna set out to comply with them.

Her bewilderment grew as the day progressed. He worked with intensity and purpose. He asked her searching questions about the inner workings of every department, then engaged key personnel in deep private discussions.

One thing she now knew for certain—Jake Rowland was no stranger to corporate dealings. And he seemed to be intent on accomplishing something more than just an impersonation of Evan. What? Was he simply trying to set things right after the embezzlement? Cy had said it would take time and analysis to know how the manipulations had affected the company. But why would Jake launch an "idea drive" and motivate employees with public recognition?

He worked through lunch, conducting his conferences late into the afternoon. Brianna spent every minute she could catching up on her own work. Around four, he called her into his office again.

"Have a seat." He gestured to the chair beside his desk. "As a key employee, I'm sure you have opinions about what's good and bad with the company. Let's hear 'em."

She regarded him in astonishment. "You really want to know what I think?"

"Yes, Ms. Devon, I do."

Not one to let an opportunity slide, she obliged him. She told him about the tension between departments, which she believed came from pressure to sell insurance policies that the underwriters and engineers considered too risky. Other departments also felt under the gun to compromise their work, in an effort to make the product more competitive for sales. Jake listened and questioned her with the same purposeful intensity she'd noticed before.

Maude interrupted, handed Jake the idea box from the break room and informed him it was quitting time. He encouraged her to go home, then remained at his desk, riffling through the suggestions.

One caught Brianna's eye. It sported a lipstick red outline of lips puckered for a kiss. Arching a brow, she picked up the slip and studied it. "You're sure to find this one interesting."

He looked up from the entries he was scanning.

She read aloud the suggestion written beside the scarlet lip print. "CEO should work the night shift with me some time soon."

He set the slips he'd been reading aside. "Who wrote it?"

"Sorry. It's not signed."

Leveling her a heavy-lidded stare, he queried, "Do you think I care whether or not it's signed? Do you think I have any interest in following up on that offer?"

She wasn't sure how to answer him. A few flip remarks came to mind, but she sensed a seriousness behind his lightly posed question.

He leaned forward on his desk, studying her face at closer range. "Do you think I'm flattered by the attention, Brianna, or aroused by the implied invitation?"

She resorted to honesty and held up her hands in a shrug. "I don't know. I could understand why you might be."

A sardonic smile twisted his mouth. "My grandfather gets offers like these from women younger than you. My great-aunt was in her seventies and bedridden, yet she had studs writing her love letters. Every member of the illustrious Rowland family has been plied with offers of all kinds for as long as I can remember." With his elbow on the desk, he leaned his chin on his fist. "What do you think they're after, all these admirers languishing after my attention?"

Taken aback by the cynicism she'd never before seen in him, she asked in surprise, "You think they're after your *money?*" She hadn't thought of that aspect of the invitation at all—or the idea that it might bother him.

He sat back and shrugged, his cynicism giving way to indifference. "Money, power, notoriety or just an old-fashioned good time. I'm sure not opposed to that." To her relief, the hint of a renegade twinkle returned to his eyes. "Then, of course, there are the ones who are really overcome by my personal appeal."

"I'm glad," she whispered, meaning it.

He stared at her, his expression gradually turning intense. "The only one I want is you, Brianna. Tonight."

She drew back from him, too overcome by the personal appeal he'd just described. This was the man she'd run from, all those years, whose wicked gaze had always set her pulse thrumming. "I...I have work to do tonight. A lot of it."

"So do I. I have to meet with the computer crew. Might take me a while. I'll come by whenever I get away."

"I'll be too tired. It's been a long day."

"We'll take a hot shower. I'll give you a massage."

It sounded like sheer heaven. She shook her head in mild panic and stood up. Another night would only make her feel closer to him. That would never do. "I'd probably fall asleep before you got there."

"Then, I'll just sleep with you."

Emotions collided within her. She wanted very much to do all those things he'd mentioned. "Not tonight." She turned away. "I'd better gather my work to take home." Hastily she retreated to her own office.

As she shoved paperwork into her briefcase, she realized he stood in the doorway, watching her. "Does this have anything to do with those inhibitions I'm supposed to be helping you lose?"

"No! Not at all."

He sauntered closer. "I didn't notice any inhibitions last night."

Her face warmed, and she admitted, "Neither did I."

She forced a wretched smile. "You must have helped me, Jake, just as you promised. I'm over them. Thank you!" Closing her briefcase, she locked it and grabbed her coat from the coat tree.

He caught her arm, turned her to face him. "As proud as that makes me feel," he drawled, "I don't believe a damn word of it." His hands traveled to her shoulders, warming her, holding her. "You're running scared and I want to know why."

"I'm not scared. I'm just—"

"Tired," he finished. Sweeping his hands in a slow path down her back, he pressed her against his hard, muscular body, reminding her of last night's loving. "Let Dr. Jake remedy that," he whispered. And he brushed a kiss across the corner of her mouth.

Sensations tingled from that featherlight kiss, taking her by surprise. He took advantage of her parted lips, this time swiping his tongue across her bottom lip.

A trembling started in her knees. He caught her against him in a harder embrace and slanted his mouth, delving with a force that thrilled her. Her arms came up around him and she countered every move of his tongue, eliciting a moan from deep within him.

The kiss grew rough, a little desperate, ending when he braced his thumbs alongside her mouth and forced himself away, his gaze hot, his whisper gruff. "I'll be at your house by nine."

8

HIS WORK WITH the computer crew kept Jake later than he'd expected, and he drove to Brianna's house wondering if she'd let him in. Their kiss at the office had left him with a compelling hunger for her, but he knew she hadn't fully approved of his visit from the start. The delay might have given her time to change her mind.

Open your door to me, Brianna. He knocked and waited on her front porch, his insides tightly coiled. *Open to me.*

Warmth, light and some succulent aroma engulfed him as the door opened. She wore jeans and a soft peach-colored sweatshirt, her hair loose about her shoulders, her eyes cautious and uncertain. Nonetheless, she let him in and took him to her kitchen, where she had a homemade supper of chicken and rice waiting. He'd almost forgotten the pleasure of a home-cooked meal—something he rarely had nowadays.

It touched him, that she'd thought he might be hungry. He was. He hadn't wanted to waste time stopping somewhere, when he knew he could be with her.

They barely said a word while he ate. She sat at the table with him, nursing a glass of wine and trying to avoid his stare. She looked soft and vulnerable and so damned beautiful he had a hard time swallowing. He wondered if she needed wine to relax. He drank deeply from the glass she'd poured him, hoping it might take the edge off his own need.

He wanted to go slowly with her tonight.

He started them with a shower. She was hesitant and shy at first, entering the bathroom in a fluffy white robe sashed at her narrow waist. He undressed himself with deliberate languor, watching her watch him. He stripped off his shirt, his jeans, his underwear. His desire for her stood in plain bold view. She looked away, her color high.

"Take off your robe," he instructed in a tight whisper.

Steam from the running shower misted, dreamlike, around her. Brianna bent her head to untie her sash, her hair falling over her eyes, her fingers trembling as she worked at the knot. He looked so dark, huge and savage in his nakedness, his body tightly muscled and primed for her. She knew the strength of that body. She knew its power.

Wicked sensuality curled through her, overcoming her shyness. She let the robe drop to the floor.

Muscles moved in his arms, chest and jaw. His gaze darkened, moving over her with probing heat. "Come here."

She stepped closer. He drew her into the pulsating heat of the shower, where he lathered soap over every curve and cleft of her body, his slow, hard hands setting fires in her blood. She took pleasure in soaping him—his sinewy arms and chest, his lean hips and abdomen, and lower.

Their mouths merged in steamy kisses. Passion grew intense. With strong, urgent hands he lifted her, and they made love right there, against the shower wall, as hot water beat against his back and sluiced down their bodies.

They came together in a blinding release, and realization flashed through her. She'd make love this way to no other man. No one else could work her into such sweet desperation. Only Jake.

No truth had ever scared her more.

But there it was, and here he was, holding her tightly against his thundering heart. Why, why should Jake be the one to ignite her passion? He played at life and love with reckless abandon, as if they were mere games. She could never expect more from him than this wild pleasure ride.

Yet she wanted this pleasure ride. She saw no sense in running from him or from her desire. She'd tried since the day they had met. But he'd played havoc with her subconscious, interfering with relationships that would have been so much better for her peace of mind.

She'd have to be stronger now than ever. Strong enough to face the fire and let their passion burn as hot and fierce as it could.

Until it had all burned out.

THE DAY HAD STARTED better than any in his life. Jake had opened his eyes to find Brianna curved against him. He'd woken her with long leisurely kisses.

The lovemaking just kept getting better.

That alone mystified him, along with the emotion that grabbed him whenever he thought about her. She was no longer the woman he hadn't had, the one who'd gotten away, the grass that looked so much greener on the other side of the hill.

He'd played on that grassy hillside. It really *was* the greenest, the deepest, the most lush and fragrant he'd ever known. But he couldn't dwell on that discovery...not if he wanted to keep it light.

She rode to work with him, venturing out into the brisk winds of the season's first heavy snowfall. As snow caked on the windshield between quick sweeps of the wipers, Jake navigated the car around a slippery curve. "Do you have good snow tires on your car?" he asked her.

She hesitated a little too long. "The tires are fine."

"Why haven't I seen you driving a car?" He hadn't thought about that fact until now.

"Mine's in the shop. The engine's being rebuilt. They're having a problem getting some of the parts."

"You don't still have that old sedan you bought in college, do you?"

"There's nothing wrong with it that can't be fixed."

"You've had it for ten years. Why not buy a new one?"

"I don't see the point. It's completely paid off. My house is close enough to town that I can walk anywhere."

"In snow like this?"

"I could have called a friend."

"What about when you work late at the office? Do you walk home alone after dark?"

"If I feel like it."

An unfamiliar sensation reached into him, like a cold, shadowy hand hovering above a vital organ. Even in towns as small as Pleasantville, women could be assaulted walking alone at night. "Are you saying you can't afford a car?"

"Of course I can afford a car. If I wanted a new one, I'd work it into my budget. I happen to think it's more important to pay off my mortgage sooner and build up a bank account to fall back on in case of...in case I... Really, Jake, this is none of your business!"

He didn't press for an answer. He saw the stubborn tilt to her chin, the militant squaring of her shoulders.

He'd never known a woman more set on doing things her own way.

He supposed he understood that. He'd walked out of his grandfather's house on the threat of being disinherited for the same reason; he intended to live life his way. An inheritance from his parents gave him a good start. Brianna hadn't had that advantage. But she'd put herself through college and bought a nice house in the historic district of town. It couldn't have been easy.

She deserved to have more. He wanted to give her more.

"What about your charity work?" he reminded her. "Food and clothing drives, toys at Christmas. You still do those?"

"Well, yes. It *would* be easier working with the kids if my car ran," Brianna admitted. Her lack of transportation actually bothered her a great deal this time of year. She wanted to be doing more than making phone calls in their drive to collect coats and boots for the poor. She would have liked to personally visit the kids and take them to weekend festivals and ball games. They needed a little time away from their dreary home lives. She'd been in their situation for a brief, terrifying time. She knew their desperation.

"Which kids are you working with now?" he asked.

"The ones in our community who don't have much or go many places without someone who can—" She broke off, hesitant to get started on a subject so close to her heart. She was feeling particularly vulnerable this morning and didn't want to engage her emotions about anything too deeply. "My car will be working soon," she insisted, drawing the topic to a determined close.

"Until then, you can use mine. It's just sitting in the garage while I'm driving Evan's."

"Your black Maserati?" she asked, amazed that he'd offered. The small sleek car had probably cost more than her beloved house.

"What's wrong with it?"

She bit her lip to stop a laugh. She'd be the envy of every guy in town if she drove that car. The women would be peeved to think Jake Rowland had given it to her to drive. Wouldn't the rumors fly! She couldn't consider it. "The kids would get a charge out of it, that's for sure," she mused, keeping her sarcasm mild. "I could probably fit two little ones in the passenger seat, on an older one's lap. The trick would be getting them all into seat belts, especially the three I'd have to carry on the roof."

"At least it's transportation."

"I can't drive your car around town. Too many people would recognize it. They'd wonder why I was driving it. You're not supposed to be here, remember? I don't like borrowing cars, anyway. I'll just wait for my own."

She was relieved when he nodded in acceptance of her decision. Only then did she silently concede that it had been kind of him to worry about her. Again, she realized how different he was proving to be than she'd expected. But she didn't want him to be kind. Passionate, yes. Kind, no.

She didn't want to blur the line she'd drawn in the sand.

BY NOON, HER VOICE mail was full of messages from supervisors insisting she call them. She'd been visited by employees from every department and the universal question seemed to be: Is it true that Mr. Rowland is putting the changes into effect that he announced this morning?

While she'd been working on employee benefits, Jake had met with department heads. Unable to speak with him because of his busy schedule, she left a message for him.

He called her into his office at noon. "Did you want to see me, Ms. Devon?"

"Yes sir, Mr. Rowland, I do." As soon as she'd closed and locked the door behind her, she rounded on him. "I'd like to know what the hell you're doing. Why did you announce those changes? You can't really put them into effect." His old colors seemed to be shining again—mischief and mayhem in eye-catching hues.

Dropping a pen onto his desk, he leaned back in his chair and lifted a brow. "Which changes don't you like?"

"It's not that I don't like them. Of course I like them. Where did they come from—the idea box?"

"So it would seem."

She stared at him in consternation. "Answer me, Jake."

"Ideas I've chosen will go into effect next week. Sales reps can work from their homes and cars instead of from the office. Their sales figures will decide whether they're doing a good job. Once they're set up at home, the company will need less work space here and have lower utility bills."

The neat logic came as a surprise to her. "Okay, I can understand the sales reps working from their homes and cars, but what about the clerical staff? I've heard you're planning to let some secretaries work from home, too."

"Why not? As long as their bosses don't have special projects that require their presence, I see no reason they can't produce the same work from home. Computers, phone systems and fax machines make that possible."

"And job sharing?" She was almost afraid to ask about it, so fervently had she wanted that particular program. Working mothers had begged her to let them share jobs to spend more time with their families.

"As long as only one of the two employees sharing a position needs benefits, I don't see how it would hurt."

"Oh, it wouldn't hurt the company," she assured him. "Most of the ones who want to share jobs have benefits through their spouse's employer."

He smiled at her, and her confusion deepened.

"*Can* you make these changes? You're here to impersonate Evan. Has he given you permission?"

"I've talked to him." His voice and expression hardened almost imperceptibly. "He knows what I'm doing."

"Will the board allow you to make these changes?"

"I have all the authorization I need." His tone left no room for question. She supposed she shouldn't worry about the changes, since he had approval from Evan and the board. "Brianna, the changes we've just discussed are ones that will be popular with the employees. But we're going to have to make a few others that won't be."

"Oh?" She sank down into the seat beside his desk, thoroughly worried now. "What changes?"

"Some of our bigger commercial accounts will have to be sold to other insurance companies."

"Why?" she asked with concerned dismay. "The sales reps make big commissions off those accounts. That could cut a lot of salaries by more than half."

"Our cash reserve is too low to handle the risk. If even one of those big accounts puts in a catastrophic claim, we won't be able to cover the loss."

"Because of the embezzlement?"

Jake hesitated. He didn't want to lie. The theft had

nothing to do with this problem. Evan's poor judgment had caused the dangerous imbalance of risk against reserve. "Evan could explain the specifics better than I can."

She nodded, and Jake knew she assumed that Evan was more proficient in business than he. Although his ego couldn't help throbbing a little, he didn't disillusion her. He had promised Evan not to tell her about his mistakes. He couldn't break that promise. In a world where no one could be fully trusted, he and Evan had always relied on each other. He'd never knowingly hurt his twin in any way. Their bond was the one thing he'd never take lightly.

"If we cut those large accounts," Brianna pondered, "will we have to cut jobs, too?" She asked the question in the same tone a mother might use, asking a surgeon, "Will my baby's leg have to be amputated?"

He realized, then, the impact the possible layoffs would have on her as human resources director. She'd be trapped in the role she'd like the least—having to personally wield the ax when employees had to be dismissed. He didn't want to put her through that, but business was business. The solvency of the company hung in the balance.

"If we cut those large accounts," he replied, carefully wording his evasion of her question, "some sales reps might choose to go with another company." Consulting his watch, he interrupted her murmurs of concern with, "It's twelve-thirty. Let's go to lunch."

That managed to divert her. She went to get her coat.

Jake, meanwhile, buzzed Maude. "Did that delivery arrive?"

"Yes, sir."

He hoped the surprise he had waiting for Brianna in

the parking lot would brighten her spirits. They'd need brightening in the weeks to come.

"WHAT DO YOU mean, it's mine?"

"It's yours," Jake repeated, as if that had fully answered her question. "How do you like it?"

Brianna gaped wordlessly at the sleek gray minivan parked in the snow-covered lot.

"You can fit seven kids in without a problem," he pointed out as he unlocked the driver's door and gave her the keys. "Get in. Let's take her for a spin."

Aware that others might overhear, she looked around and noticed a few of her co-workers on the sidewalk headed for the local diner. In a harsh undertone, she said, "I can't buy this car!"

"I didn't ask you to buy it."

"You want me to *borrow* it?"

"No, not borrow. You already said you wouldn't. Think of it as a company car."

"But it's not a company car. My position doesn't warrant one. It wasn't paid for with company funds, was it?"

"No, but—"

"Thanks, but no thanks." She tossed the keys to him and shoved the door closed without so much as glancing inside. Its interior would be plush, she knew. This make and model was far more expensive than anything she'd buy for herself. And he was right about the kids fitting in nicely. They'd each have a seat belt. If only she could afford to buy it herself without blowing her budget. "Take it back."

He pocketed the keys she'd thrown him and followed her across the parking lot. "Brianna, you need a good car. This one's reliable and gets fairly good gas mileage. It's rated high for safety, and its resale value is sound."

Afraid that co-workers might overhear, she stopped beside Evan's Mercedes. "Let's talk about this somewhere private."

He opened her door, climbed in his side and drove down Main Street. "You can pick out any car you'd like. We'll drive over to the dealership now."

"No, Jake! I won't be indebted to you."

"Indebted to me?" He trapped her in a solemn gaze. "I didn't realize we were keeping tabs. Do I owe you for last night's supper?"

"Don't be ridiculous. A new car isn't quite the same as chicken and rice."

"Do you think it's harder for me to buy this car than it was for you to make supper? I probably had it easier. All I had to do is pick up the phone, sign a few papers..."

"That's not the point."

"Then what is?"

She hadn't meant to hurt his feelings, but she sensed that she had. Regret filled her. But she couldn't take the car from him. It went against everything she held sacred. "If you don't want women chasing you for your money," she admonished, "you shouldn't go around buying them cars."

He squared his jaw, pulled abruptly into a parking lot behind a restaurant and turned to her with a frown. "I don't want advice from you about women. But just to set the record straight, I've never bought a car for anyone before."

"Then don't start now."

"I'm not giving it to you because you're a woman, or because you're my...my lover." A warm rush went through her to hear him call her that. He himself fell silent for the space of a few stilted heartbeats. "I bought it because I care about what might happen to you without a good car."

"I know you mean well, but I...I can't." She got out of the car, feeling the need for space.

He soon fell into step behind her as she headed for the restaurant. Neither said a word until they'd been seated at a corner booth partitioned off by gleaming walnut walls, stained glass windows and hanging ferns.

"If you're not going to let me buy you lunch, let me know right now," he uttered with quiet force. "You can take yours to go. I'll drive you back to the office and we can figure out how much we owe each other for the past two weeks. Divvy up expenses, estimate the value of services rendered."

"That would be fine with me."

"It wouldn't with me, damn it." The ferocity in his stare brought a lump to her throat. He wasn't going to understand a very important aspect of her life—her need for self-reliance, her need to remain out of any man's debt.

"Brianna." His voice had changed, and he reached out to take her hand. "You're not about to cry, are you?"

"Of course not." She held back the ridiculous tears with masterful control. She didn't believe he could see any more than maybe a glimmer that barely blurred her vision.

Remorse clouded his face. He let go of her hand, which she'd kept unresponsive, and sat back in his seat with a wretched sigh. "I'm sorry. I didn't mean to hurt you." He raked a hand through his hair, looking utterly despondent. "I guess I should have learned my lesson when I was ten."

"Ten?" She couldn't help responding to that. "You tried to give a woman a car when you were ten?"

"Not a car. Money." A self-mocking smile bent his lips. "She'd been our housekeeper since Evan and I were born. Mrs. Dimitri. My parents stayed away most of the time, and she...well, she did everything for us. She had a son our age. Cort, his name was. And a younger daughter. We ate meals together in the kitchen, joked and laughed. Fought sometimes—the four of us kids, I mean. We were like those families you see on TV." He paused, reminiscing. "Evan and I hadn't realized that our family was separate from theirs, let alone different in any way that mattered. The concept of rich and poor, employer and employee, hadn't really occurred to us yet." His mouth twisted with some remembered irony. "Then a kid at school called us millionaires. We weren't sure how to take that. I asked my father about it. He acted proud. Told me that a paltry million wouldn't make much difference to us, but to others it would mean a great deal." Jake's gaze focused on Brianna. "I told him and my mother that I wanted to give Mrs. Dimitri a million dollars."

She easily envisioned him as an earnest ten-year-old, intent on bettering the lives of the family he'd come to love. "That was sweet of you, Jake. I doubt anyone took your request very seriously."

"My mother did. She warned Evan and me to watch out for 'common people' who try to make you love them, because they're only after your money. She made us promise to be pleasant with the 'help,' as she called the Dimitris, but not to get too attached. The next weekend she sent us away to a friend's house. When we came home..." he paused, his lips pressed together "...Mrs. Dimitri had moved out. She'd been fired."

Brianna's throat worked to dislodge a sudden ache. She had to hide her compassion from him. She knew instinctively that he wouldn't welcome it. As blandly as she could, she asked, "Did you see her after that?"

He shook his head. "They packed up and moved out of town, I guess." His stare slipped out of focus. "I never heard from them again."

When the heaviest part of the silence had passed, Brianna reached for his hand and covered it. "They might have tried. Your mother might have intercepted mail or kept phone calls from you."

He blinked, his reverie disrupted, then shrugged as if he didn't care much. "Maybe. But don't think too badly of my mother. Before that, one of the maids filed a paternity suit against my father. Tests proved he wasn't responsible, but..." Jake forced a smile "...my mother never trusted the 'help' after that. She never trusted anyone. Couldn't blame her. A family friend sold photos of my father with the maid. A tabloid paid ten thousand for the pictures. A buck's a buck."

Brianna bit her bottom lip and looked down at her hand now clasped in his. How betrayed his family must have felt! "Your parents were killed in an accident, weren't they?"

"A yachting accident."

"How old were you then?"

"Twelve."

A ponderous silence overtook them as a waitress set menus on their table. Brianna wished she could comfort herself with the knowledge that his grandfather had been there for him. But as she thought back to her highschool friendship with Evan, she remembered that Cy had rarely been home. He hadn't known his grandsons' friends or attended school activities, as far as she could remember.

Jake squeezed her hand. "Hey, I'm sorry. I didn't

mean to ruin your lunch hour. Evan and I got along fine. We looked out for each other."

By the way he said it, she knew how close the two must have been. That realization didn't go very far in lightening her spirits, but to please Jake she forced a smile.

A tenderness came into his gaze that made her heart trip over itself. "I'll send the car back," he promised. "We'll forget I ever brought the subject up." He studied her eyes, a question in his. "Won't we?"

She nodded.

"If you want," he said in a cautious, tentative way, "you can use Evan's Mercedes while I'm gone. I've got to fly to Boston tonight and meet with another insurance company that might buy those large accounts we talked about."

"You're leaving tonight?" She didn't know why that news surprised her. Evan had gone on business trips every few weeks; she'd come to expect them as part of their usual routine. "How long will you be gone?"

"I should be back by next Wednesday."

A whole week. She glanced away from him, struggling to hide her disappointment that he was leaving. The time he'd be gone stretched before her like an empty chasm. Since when did one week seem so long? Since when did she hate for Jake Rowland to leave her? "Thanks, but I won't need the car."

He looked as if he might say more. Instead, he bowed his head and studied the menu with intense concentration.

JAKE WENT HOME after work and packed, wishing he didn't have to leave. He'd hurt Brianna today in a way he hadn't understood. He wanted the chance to hold her, talk to her, find out why she'd cried over that damned car...and, of course, to make love to her. Sleep with her. Wake up in her arms.

What the hell was happening to him? His time suddenly seemed divided into only two categories—time spent with Brianna, and time spent waiting to be with her. She was like an addictive drug. The more he sampled, the more he craved.

She had him feeling things he'd never felt, doing things he'd never done—like trying to force cars on unwilling women—and saying things he'd never intended to say. Like telling her about the Dimitris. He hadn't mentioned their names since they'd left. Why had he brought them up now?

You're not taking this affair with her as lightly as you should.

He locked his suitcase and noticed the message light on the phone beside his bed. He pressed the *play* button.

"Jake, I have only a minute in private." Evan's voice sounded hushed and hurried. "Things are looking up. That detective you hired has a few leads on Cassandra. Oh, and uh, listen, Jake, when I told you that Brianna and I had broken up...well, I might have been a little hasty. Don't try putting any moves on her, okay? I imagine you're bored to death by now and looking for a little diversion. Not that she'd have your sorry butt." His chuckle sounded a little strained. "She's probably ready to kill you, if I know the two of you. Anyway, if and when I get out of this embezzlement mess, I...I want Brianna back."

9

"So, DID MY candlelight dinner do the trick?" Chloe asked as she helped herself to Brianna's leftover chicken and rice.

Brianna pushed the food around her own plate without eating. It was Sunday evening—Jake had been gone only four days—yet she missed him enough to call Chloe over to spend the night, something she hadn't done in years.

She wished she could tell her that Evan had broken up with her, but then how could she explain Jake's presence without giving away the impersonation? She'd given Cy Rowland her word to tell no one, and she couldn't go back on her word. "Chloe, things are complicated right now between us. I'd rather not talk about Evan."

"I knew something had to be wrong. But I can't believe that nothing came of last Monday night's dinner."

She couldn't evade Chloe's perceptive gaze for long and soon felt a blush rise up her neck.

"Something *did* come of it, didn't it?" deduced Chloe. "You finally went to bed with him. That's what we've been shooting for, isn't it?" She narrowed her eyes. "Don't tell me you didn't like it."

"I didn't say that."

"So did you?"

Brianna set down her fork, drew in a deep breath and

gazed at the ceiling. "Yes," she conceded in a drawn-out whisper. "I liked it." *Too much.*

Chloe studied her in puzzlement. "I figured you would, especially after I saw you two at the restaurant. He seemed a lot sexier than he ever has before. And you were kind of—I don't know—glowing."

Setting her elbows on the table, Brianna buried her face in her hands. How could she miss Jake when he'd been gone only four days? When Evan had gone out of town, even for weeks at a time, she simply used that time to get things done. She hadn't counted the hours until he returned, or gotten distracted in her work with ideas of how to welcome him home. "I thought we weren't going to talk about this," she mumbled through her fingers.

"But if the sex was good, why are you moping?"

Brianna lowered her hands from her face. "I'm not moping. I'm confused. I'm not sure how I feel about...about Evan." Of course she really meant Jake. She couldn't get too attached to him! He distracted her too much from the important things. And he'd be leaving when Evan returned.

"Where's Evan now?" Chloe asked.

"Out of town on business."

"*That's* your problem. You both work too much. All work and no play makes Jack and Jill a dull couple. I have an idea! You know what's coming up, don't you?"

"No." Brianna suspected she didn't want to know, either. "What?"

"My birthday is Friday and Evan's is Saturday."

"That's right, it is. How do *you* know Evan's birthday?"

"It's the day after mine. Every year we used to hand out lollipops in elementary school—me first, then him."

Guilt descended on Brianna. Evan would spend his birthday alone, held against his will in France. How could she have been so wrapped up in Jake as to forget about Evan's anguish? He'd been a good friend to her for many years. With surprise, she realized the nature of her feelings for him—*sisterly*. Why hadn't she seen that before? She wanted to call him, talk to him, comfort him, but Cy had forbidden all contact...*and* she didn't have a phone number for him.

"Hey, I'm not thrilled about having another birthday myself, but let's not mourn over it." Chloe munched on a bread stick. "I think we should throw a party. We'll hold it Saturday night at my house."

"I'd love to celebrate your birthday, Chloe, but the way things are with Evan and me—"

"I'll invite the guests. All my friends know I'm shameless enough to throw myself a birthday party. We'll keep it a surprise for Evan, though. I love surprises. All you have to do is get him there." With another glance at Brianna, Chloe's expression fell. "Of course, if you don't *want* to celebrate my birthday, we don't have to." Rising from the table with a distinct sniff, she carried her dishes to the sink, looking very much the martyr.

Brianna doubted that Chloe's feelings were really hurt. At least, she didn't *think* they were.

"I haven't had a birthday party since I was a kid," Chloe mumbled, rinsing the plate. "Thought it might be fun. But if you're too busy, or too wrapped up in Evan..."

"Okay, Chloe," Brianna relented, "I'll come to your party. But I'm not sure if I can bring Evan."

"If you don't bring him, I'll find a way to get him there. I can be very inventive, you know."

Foreboding filled Brianna. Jake had passed as Evan at

the office because Maude and she ran interference, screening his calls and visits, filling him in on anything Evan should know. What would happen at an intimate gathering of friends? He wouldn't know most of them; they weren't his kind of crowd. The impersonation could be blown.

She'd have to warn Jake. Maybe he could give Chloe some excuse that she'd accept. From the determined sparkle in Chloe's brown eyes, though, Brianna guessed that it would have to be one doozy of an excuse.

ALONE IN A BOSTON hotel suite, Jake ordered a bottle of Jack Daniels from room service, grabbed the TV's remote control and switched to the Tuesday night movie. He'd had invitations from his business associates for every evening—one an attractive female who was obviously in heat—but he'd declined.

He was in no mood for company, unless that company happened to be Brianna. Which, of course, it couldn't be. She was hundreds of miles away from him, and not only in the physical sense. Much more than distance separated them.

Evan wanted her back.

Jake cursed and turned off the television. Why the hell had Evan waited so long to decide he missed her? If Evan had told Jake how he felt about her during that first phone call, Jake never would have gone after her. Never would have taken her to bed, never would have gotten hooked on making love to her.

That's a crock. You'd have done it anyway.

He honestly didn't know if he would have or not. He'd always considered Evan and Brianna to be friends, platonic friends. Her claim that they'd been dating had taken him by surprise, like a pit bull going for his throat.

But then Evan had broken up with her, and she'd become fair game.

Jake paced across the hotel room, caught in an inner crossfire. Who was he kidding? He couldn't pursue Brianna if his brother loved her.

Maybe she wouldn't want Evan. Maybe the intimacies she'd shared with him, Jake, had changed her mind. Then again, maybe not. He leaned his forehead against the cold plate-glass window that overlooked the Boston skyline and forced from his mind the worst scenarios.

Keep it light. Hadn't he learned that lesson by now? Life didn't hurt as much once that skill was mastered. He simply had to lighten his attitude toward this whole ordeal.

He needed to talk to Evan, to ask him about his feelings for Brianna and base his actions on that. But what could he say if Evan *did* love her? *Sorry, but she and I have wild sex every chance we get. I'd really like to keep on with that. Hope you don't mind too much, bro.*

No, he couldn't discuss the matter with Evan yet. But he could call Brianna. To keep peace with his conscience, he'd managed to resist calling her for almost a full week.

The clock on the bedside table read eleven-fifteen. She might still be awake. He could let her know the good news about the business, and of course, that he'd be away longer than he'd planned.

He *had* to call her. He needed to hear her voice again.

She answered on the second ring with a soft, sleepy, "Hello?"

"Hello, yourself."

"Jake! Where are you?" Her warmth eased something inside of him, but only for a moment. Would her welcome turn to awkwardness when she knew Evan wanted her back?

"I'm in Boston." He supposed he should tell her about Evan's message—and gauge her feelings by her reply—but he didn't think he could deal with that issue right now with the necessary objectivity. "The computer crew came through for us. I talked to Irene Cahn today. They've corrected the embezzler's manipulations in the system. Our customers' accounts are balanced, and chances of an investigation here in the States are now slim to none."

"That's wonderful!" Her gladness made the news even more satisfying than it had been when he'd heard it himself.

"Things are coming along okay here in Boston, too, but it looks like I'll be stuck here longer than I'd planned."

"Oh." Was that disappointment he heard? He couldn't be sure. *Was she missing him?* "When will you get back?"

"Late Saturday, maybe even Sunday."

"Ah." She paused. "Well..."

He waited for her to finish her reply, but she didn't. The silence seemed charged, as if she were groping for something to say. He closed his eyes. He wanted to be there with her so badly. When he finally broke the silence, he asked in a voice a little too hoarse, "Are you in bed?"

"Yes."

The image of her appeared to him so vibrant and clear that it made him ache. "Have you taken your shower yet?" He had no business asking her that, no business thinking about the shower they'd taken together, the love they'd made.

"I took a bath."

"Ah." He paused. "Well..." He gazed blindly at the

far wall, imagining what he had missed by being away. He couldn't go on like this! He was driving himself nuts. *Keep it light.* Jokingly he queried, "So, do you miss me?"

Seconds ticked by as he waited for her rejoinder, and he found himself swallowing against a dry throat. It wasn't as if he hadn't asked that question to hundreds of women, sometimes the day after a casual date, just to be cute, just to hear them breathe flirtatious things into the receiver like *Desperately* or *You know I do, honey...*

"It's only been a few days." She hadn't answered right. He hadn't even heard a smile in her voice.

He couldn't quite manage one, either. "That's not what I asked."

In a barely audible murmur, she allowed, "I wouldn't mind if you were here."

He shut his eyes. "I wouldn't mind being there."

Again, the almost painful silence. He was afraid she might say goodbye. Crazy to stay on a long-distance line and say nothing. But he didn't want to break their connection, even a silent one.

She cleared her throat and came to their rescue. "In case you get back early enough on Saturday, I guess I'd better tell you—Chloe is throwing a party for her and Evan."

"Her and Evan?" That certainly helped to distract him from the longing that was gnawing at his gut.

"Her birthday is Friday and his is Saturday." *His*, she'd said. Not *yours*, as in, Evan's and Jake's. She seemed to have forgotten he was Evan's twin—almost as if she'd forgotten he existed outside the impersonation. Oblivious to her omission, she went on, "She's invited our closest friends. She wants to surprise Evan." A note of relief crept into her voice. "But since you're coming in too late, we won't have to worry about it."

Jake frowned. He didn't like her putting a positive spin on his absence. "Are you going?"

"I promised Chloe I would."

"But you don't want...Evan...to show up for his own party."

She let out a little laugh. "Evan himself would be okay. I'm not too sure about you."

Jake set his teeth on edge. He couldn't let an unacknowledged birthday or a simple comment get under his skin; she'd said a lot worse over the years. He couldn't let the woman herself get under his skin. "Then I guess it's a good thing that I probably won't be there in time."

A different kind of silence followed his quiet remark.

"Jake? Is something...wrong?"

"Wrong? Not at all. But it's been a long day and I'm, uh, ready to turn in."

"Ah. Well..." She paused. "Good night."

He forced out a cool, "Good night."

HE LANDED AT the Columbus airport around seven on Saturday evening and drove to Pleasantville. His trip, although successful, had been hell. He hadn't slept much. Hadn't eaten much. Hadn't even bothered drinking much, barely touching the Jack Daniels he'd ordered from room service. Nothing seemed to satisfy. Nothing helped lighten the heaviness pressing down on him.

He had to give up Brianna...at least until he knew whether or not she and Evan loved each other. After all the justifications he'd found to keep on seeing her, he couldn't betray his brother that way.

The question that nagged at him was, *did* Evan really love her? If so, why hadn't he said it when Jake asked him about her? Evan could have been angry with her at the time, he supposed. Brianna had mentioned that they'd had a fight. She'd also written about those mysterious inhibitions that blocked them from intimacy—inhibitions he himself hadn't seen a sign of. Evan might have given up on their relationship, then thought better of it.

Something about that didn't ring true to Jake. If Brianna were his, no amount of anger or frustration would make him tell another man that he was finished with her. If a man even hinted at an interest in her, he'd tell the bastard to keep his hands off her or risk death. Above all, no fight with her or problem in bed would lead him to break off their relationship.

Evan had been a fool to let her go...*if* he loved her.

Then again, Evan had been acting like a fool about everything lately. Letting his business run into trouble and an embezzler walk off with his cash. Was a troubled love life the cause of his preoccupation? Jake wished he knew.

The other question that nagged at Jake disturbed him even more. Did *Brianna* love *Evan*? She'd come to his apartment to make up. She'd written him a letter asking for another chance. But if her love for Evan was so damned true, why had she gone to bed with his brother?

He'd promised to help her overcome sexual problems, but he found it hard to believe that she would turn anywhere outside of her relationship with Evan to solve them...if she really loved him. That wasn't the Brianna he knew. When he held her, when he loved her, he felt in his blood and in his bones that she belonged to him.

But she didn't. And he couldn't go to her, couldn't love her again, until he knew he was right in doing so.

Please, God, make it right.

Shortly after eight o'clock, Jake pulled into the garage

of his town house. It wouldn't be easy staying home this evening when he knew he could be with her at the party...and afterward. He'd just have to try not to think of her.

Not a great way to spend the evening of his birthday.

As he locked the door of Evan's Mercedes, a slight form approached in the shadows outside of his garage. A woman. She wore a black vinyl coat and spike-heeled boots. "Evan?"

Jake pocketed his keys and stepped forward to see her face better by the dim glow of a street lamp. "Yes?"

"Oh, Evan!" Before he had a chance to see her clearly, she threw herself against him in a fierce hug.

10

STAGGERING SLIGHTLY from the unexpected impact, Jake gaped down at the stranger in his arms. She looked to be in her early twenties, petite, with long dark hair and exotically made-up eyes. "I missed you so much," she whispered. "I've been *burning* for you. I didn't think I'd ever get away." Her lashes lowered and she leaned in for a kiss.

He pulled back with awkward dismay. What the hell to do now? He couldn't compromise the impersonation by admitting he wasn't Evan.

She opened her eyes, looking bewildered. "Are you angry with me? I'm sorry I haven't called you for so long. My husband's been in town for weeks. He finally left for his hunting cabin. I tried last night and today to reach you." Her voice lowered in a nervous whisper. "Have you broken up with Brianna yet?"

Jake blinked. "Did you expect me to?"

"You said you would." She pulled back from their loose embrace and studied him with displeasure. "You're waiting for me to tell Mike first, aren't you? Don't you believe I'm serious about our relationship?"

"Are you?" he responded, highly curious.

"I *live* for the times we're together. But it isn't easy to ask for a divorce, even in a marriage like mine." Frowning, she tilted her head. "If I leave Mike, you...you *will* still want me, won't you?"

Jake decided he'd better take control of the situation, and fast. "I'll tell you what I want." He loomed closer, his gaze direct. "I want you to go home and think long and hard about your reasons for leaving Mike."

She raised her brows in surprise.

"Don't do it just because of me," he said. Taking her by the shoulders, he ushered her toward a car parked down the street, hoping it was hers. "Ask yourself this—if I disappeared tomorrow, would you still want the divorce?"

She opened her mouth to reply.

He held up a hand. "Uh-uh...don't answer me now. Go home and think about it. Take your time—at least a few weeks." He stopped beside the parked car. "If you feel the same way then as you do now, we'll talk about us."

Her lips twitched, her eyes grew shiny. In another moment, she'd be in tears. Steeling himself against them, he turned his back on her and walked away. With great relief, he heard a door slam and a car drive off.

He climbed the stairs to his town house in a daze. Evan had been cheating on Brianna. Why the hell would any man want another woman when he could have Brianna? Anger burned in him as he thought of how hurt she'd be if she found out. If Evan were here, he'd choke him.

What had gotten into him, anyway? He wasn't the womanizing type. He'd dated the same girl throughout high school and college without ever turning an eye to other women for anything beyond friendship. When it came to women, Evan really had been one of the "nice" guys.

Both angry and bewildered, Jake strode to the phone

and punched in the number to Evan's hotel. "What the hell's going on, Ev?"

"Are you talking about the investments?" Evan moaned. "They're not doing too well. I'm worried sick."

"I don't blame you. If they keep on as they are, we're in big trouble. But that's not what I'm calling about."

"Don't tell me something else is wrong, too."

"I guess that depends on whose eyes you're looking through. A cute little brunette dropped by. Came at me with a great big hug and kiss."

"Lauren!" His surprised whisper was almost reverent. "Lauren came by? What did she say?" Then with a sudden fierceness, he blurted, "You *kissed* her?"

Jake raised a brow. He'd never heard quite the same savagery in his brother's voice before. "No, I didn't kiss her. I sent her home to her husband. She said she's going to leave him for you. I can't promise that still applies."

Evan's breath hissed like a deflating balloon. "Hell."

"Hell because she's leaving her husband, or because she might change her mind?"

"I can't break up her family." Dejection darkened every word. "She has a baby. I can't do that to the kid. What would we have done if Dad had run off with the maid? Lord, Jake, I never should have gotten involved with her. But Brianna wouldn't...Brianna didn't...oh, hell. I just couldn't help it. Once I started with Lauren, I couldn't eat, couldn't sleep, couldn't think about anything else. Look what a mess I've made out of everything because of it."

"And now you want Brianna back."

"Brianna," he reflected on a sigh. "She's good for me, Jake. She helps me think straight. We work through problems like a team. I need her."

"You need a damn kick in the butt," Jake growled. "I'm not going to let you hurt Brianna."

"I'd never hurt her! That's why I broke up with her. But I've come to my senses. Lauren has to stay with her husband and I have to stay with Brianna."

"Sorry, Ev. You broke it off. As far as I'm concerned, that makes her fair game."

"Fair game? Damn it, Jake, don't start messing with—"

Click. Jake hung up the phone, and his anger gradually lost its steam. An odd exhilaration swept into its place. His duty became clear. He had to protect Brianna from a broken heart.

"I HOPE EVAN MAKES it," Chloe said for at least the third time since the party had started. "I left a message on his recorder that he should drop by if he got in before midnight. I said a new neighbor of mine wanted to meet him."

Looking proud of her own resourcefulness, Chloe moved on in her silver-spangled tunic top and black tights to shout a teasing remark at someone across the room. Neighbors and friends milled around the great room of her spacious ranch-style house, laughing, munching and toasting to her birthday.

Brianna smiled and joked, determined to present a happy face, but nothing distracted her from thoughts of Jake. Last Tuesday on the phone, she'd sworn he missed her, and yet he'd ended the call on an abrupt impersonal note. Her confusion had grown. She wished she could fast-forward time until he'd come home to her again.

Except, her home wasn't Jake's, and she wasn't the only woman in his life. He'd be leaving for foreign ports, with women waiting at each one. She had to remember that. She lost sight of it too easily these days.

It was better that he didn't come here tonight, she told herself. These people were friends of Evan's. Jake could be tripped up in his impersonation much easier here than at work.

The doorbell rang. She made a move to answer it, but Chloe stood closer. With a curious peep through the side window, Chloe cried, "It's Evan!"

Brianna's heart spun around. It had to be Jake. He was home!

Chloe dropped the curtain back into place and instructed everyone to yell "happy birthday" when he walked in. Brianna braced herself with a hand on the back of a nearby armchair. Anticipation sang through her veins, even while common sense begged her to keep her heart aloof. Her anxiety also rose at the potential complications of his impersonation. Why had he risked coming here tonight?

Chloe opened the door with cheerful greetings, and Jake stepped in. Snowflakes glistened in his wavy dark hair and along the broad shoulders of his black cashmere overcoat. Evan had worn that coat before, but not with Jake's casual, roguish style. Beneath it he wore a black T-shirt, faded jeans and soft leather boots. Even with his hair cut short and his face clean shaven he looked outlaw rugged, virile and criminally handsome.

The crowd shouted in unison, "Happy birthday!"

He put on a credible show of surprise, to Chloe's beaming delight, shaking his head in wry disapproval at the small mob who swarmed forward with comic quips about age and rowdy pats on the back.

Brianna hadn't shouted. She hung back from the front

lines, wishing the sight of him hadn't affected her with such a deep rush of bewildering emotion.

As Chloe took his coat, he uttered threats of revenge against her. Laughingly she claimed to have been an unwilling accomplice to "the brains behind the scheme."

He nodded, as if he'd guessed as much. "Where is she?" With his jaw squared in a parody of vengeful determination, he scanned the faces.

Brianna felt an almost physical jolt as his gaze locked with hers. She tried to smile, but the energy radiating between them interfered. Her knees grew weak as he approached. "You," he said in low tones. "You were behind this, weren't you?"

"No, not me. Chloe was the one who—"

"Don't try to put all the blame on Chloe." Despite the playfulness of his words, he brought her into his arms with a forceful pull, his blue gaze intense. "The penalty for conspiracy is stiff. Very stiff."

"But I—"

He wasted no more time on nonsense; he silenced her with a kiss. Not just the affectionate peck she'd expected in front of all these people, but a deep, moving proclamation. When the kiss had swirled to a final close, she'd forgotten about everyone but him.

"Boy!" Chloe exclaimed, gawking beside them. "Did I get the short end of *that* stick! I get the threats, she gets a thousand watt kiss."

Jake's mouth turned up in a grin, but he didn't loosen his arms from around Brianna. "I wouldn't want to blow your fuse, Chloe. By the way, happy birthday."

She looked at him with puzzlement. "You, too."

Brianna noticed, then, the surprised looks from all corners of the room. She realized that Evan had never kissed her that way in public. In fact, he'd never kissed her that way at all. And he'd never gazed at her with the heat and power now blazing from Jake's compelling eyes.

"How about a Scotch and soda?" Chloe asked him.

"Make that a beer, and I'll let you off without a birthday pinch."

"Try it and you won't see your next birthday." As she turned with a grin to get the beer, her gaze snapped back to him in a double take. "Since when do you drink beer?"

"Can you believe it?" Brianna found her voice out of sheer necessity. "He finally found some he likes. What's the name of that imported beer you discovered on your last business trip, *Evan?*" She emphasized his name to remind him of his role.

He narrowed his gaze at her, but rattled off some German-sounding name.

Chloe snorted. "I've never even heard of that."

"Scotch will be fine," he said. "On the rocks."

Chloe walked off to get his drink. Brianna wrapped an insistent hand around his arm and guided him to an unoccupied corner. "Did you forget your role?" she admonished when they were out of earshot. "Evan doesn't drink beer, and he doesn't trade double entendres with Chloe."

"Sorry. I got carried away." He turned her to face him and settled his arms around her, longing to feel her against him. "What else doesn't Evan do?"

"Well, he...he doesn't..." her voice dropped an octave "...he doesn't kiss me like you did. Or hold me like you are right now." She looked away, flustered. "In public, I mean."

"This isn't public. It's a private party." Jake cocked his head. "So you mean he *does* kiss you like that in private?" He couldn't keep the censure from his question. He didn't want to think of any other man kissing her at all.

"I can't tell you things like that. It wouldn't be fair to Evan."

"So he doesn't." Gladness swept through him, and he whispered heatedly, "Maybe he doesn't want you the way I do."

Her gaze returned to his, and he wondered if he'd hurt her. He hoped not, but he'd set out tonight to protect her from a broken heart. The only way to do that was to make her see that Evan wasn't the man for her.

"Evan and I have broken up, as you well know. I see no point in talking about the past. *Please* just try to behave."

"While we're on the subject of misbehaving," he drawled, tracing the curve of her face with the back of his fingers, "don't think I didn't notice your infraction. I'm going to have to charge you another penalty." Angling her face to his, he brushed his lips across her mouth.

Her eyelids fluttered in sensuous response, but she remained lucid enough to murmur, "What infraction?"

"I warned you not to call me Evan. I meant it." Breathing in her delectable scent, he kissed the tender side of her jaw. In her clingy red sweater and tight jeans, she looked too tempting to resist. He wanted to run his hands over every curve. She'd feel firm, warm and soft...

With a slow influx of breath and obvious reluctance, she pulled back from him. "I have to call you Evan. Mr. Rowland would sound ridiculous."

He forcibly reined in his burgeoning desire, and after a clarifying moment considered the predicament.

"Honey might be nice. Or sweetheart." His musings were rewarded with an appalled stare. "Or maybe shnookems."

"Shnookems! I'd never call anyone shnookems, least of all Evan." Caught by the sudden image of that, she glanced pointedly at Jake, and with a burst of laughter they came together in a huddle to stifle their hilarity. "He'd think I was n-nuts," she gasped against his quaking shoulder.

"Shnookems it's got to be," he decided.

As their mirth wound down, Chloe came up behind them and handed a drink to Jake. "Here's your Scotch, Ev. Come join our game of charades. You're always so good at it."

As Chloe turned toward the lively gathering near the fireplace, Jake slanted Brianna an apprehensive glance. He hadn't played charades much. She barely repressed a grin. The fact that she found his apprehension amusing bolstered his determination to shine.

The game commenced. Although he didn't guess many answers, his comments and performances kept the group laughing hard enough that no one seemed to notice. The game actually proved helpful in his impersonation, preventing deep conversations that might have tripped him up. Brianna helped by addressing everyone by name until he had them memorized.

Afterward, Chloe lit the candles on two decorated cakes. One read, "Happy Birthday, Evan."

A pang of awareness shot through Jake. Evan should be here at the center of this cheery group of friends who now sang as the candle flames danced. Silently he wished his twin a happy birthday—despite their little run-in—and made a vow to do everything in his power to bring him back to these people.

Urged on by whistles and cheers, Chloe blew out her candles. The crowd then demanded that Evan blow out his. "Make a wish!" someone yelled.

A wish. Jake had one ready-made. He held Brianna in his stare, the candlelight glinting in her hair and eyes like fiery stars. Burning brighter still, hotter than even the flames themselves, was his need for her to see him, to want him, as himself—Jake—instead of as a stand-in for Evan.

Intently he blew out every last candle.

While the others applauded, she stood watching him, as if she couldn't quite decide what she saw. Had it crossed her mind, he wondered, that today was also *his* birthday? Not that it mattered. It didn't. Not at all.

He held out his hand; she took it and they followed the others to the living room where gaily wrapped presents covered the coffee table. Chloe and he opened gag gifts that ranged from silly to naughty, winning chortles and hoots from the onlookers.

For the first time ever, he understood why his brother had spent most of his life in this one small community. He'd built a true home here. Jake, who traveled the world on a regular basis and knew people from almost every culture, realized now what he had given up— friends who shared his day-to-day life with an easy camaraderie...friends who knew his birthday without being told...friends who sometimes turned into the very best lovers. *Brianna.*

He couldn't let Evan have Brianna. He looked around, feeling the need to hold her. Where had she gone? The others had drifted into pairs and danced at the far corner of the great room.

As if beckoned by his will, she rounded the corner and

sat down on the sofa beside him, holding out a small, colorfully wrapped present. "One last gift to open."

"I'll take it home for Evan with the others," he said, making sure no one could overhear.

She hesitated. "Whoever brought this one might be waiting for a thank-you. Better open it now."

With a shrug, he reluctantly took the gift. He'd begun to feel too much the impostor. No card was attached, only a small square of white paper taped beside the miniature bow. The homemade tag read, "Shnookems." His gaze shot to her.

A dimple flashed in her cheek. She lifted a shoulder. "In case anyone else saw it."

"This is for...me?"

She caught her bottom lip between her teeth and nodded. "I was going to wait, but you seemed a little down."

A slow smile started from somewhere inside of him.

"Go ahead, open it," she urged. "It won't explode."

"If it does, I'll have to charge you one hell of a penalty," he warned. With his spirits strangely soaring, he ripped open the paper and uncovered a book for addresses and phone numbers. "A little black book."

He turned it over in his hands, somewhat bewildered. Was she telling him he'd need the proverbial "little black book," to get back into the swing of things when his time with her had ended? He glanced up at her in question.

"I hadn't thought of it as being a little black book," she replied dryly, "at least not in the sense you probably mean. Open it to the *D*'s."

Glad that his interpretation had been wrong, he flipped through the beginning of the alphabet. Why, he wondered, was she asking him to turn to the *D*'s? *Her* last name was Devon. Had she written her phone number in it? Was this her way of telling him to keep in touch, once he'd hit the road?

He reached the *D* section and found what he'd suspected—a phone number and address written in her hand. But they weren't hers. His brows drew together.

Dimitri, Cort. The name swam before his eyes.

"It's him," she declared. "Your friend who moved away. His mother remarried. She's not a Dimitri anymore. She's listed under the *K*'s."

In a state close to shock, Jake turned to the *K*'s and stared at the unfamiliar name and address written there. In parentheses, she'd printed, "Mrs. Dimitri."

Disbelief robbed him of speech.

"They weren't all that hard to find," she said. "Our receptionist, Ellie, has lived in this town forever and remembers everything that happened in it. When I asked her about the Dimitris, she said that they'd moved to Atlanta. I hit the jackpot with the third 'C. Dimitri' I called."

A great hot ball of emotion rolled up into Jake's throat and burned like the sun throughout his chest. She'd gone to all that trouble for him—to right an old wrong, to heal an old wound. To surprise him for his birthday.

He turned to her with eyes that had to be shining.

He loved her. He loved her fiercely—more than he thought humanly possible—and if he couldn't kiss her now, he'd explode.

He pulled her into his arms and submerged them into a kiss as deep and strong as the feelings coursing through him. He'd never ridden this current before, never sped headlong into this vast unknown, and he thrilled to the sensation. She sped along with him, sleek and powerful and humming, leaving the world far, far behind....

"Ahem. Excuse me." Chloe's droning voice and a sharp poke at his shoulder ejected Jake cruelly from the ride. She stood beside the sofa with her arms crossed. "May I please talk to you in private for a moment...Evan?"

Still dazed from their kiss, Jake muttered, "You have a lousy sense of timing, Chloe."

"*Now*," she insisted, drawing frowns from him and Brianna. "Bri, dear, our guests have been leaving in a steady flow. Wouldn't you like to say your goodbyes?

"Yes, of course!" The heat they'd been stoking only moments before now burned in her face as she hurried toward the departing couples.

Chloe, meanwhile, led Jake to her bedroom and to his surprise shut the door and rounded on him with a savage scowl. "You've gone too far this time, you scumbag!"

Jake blinked, startled by her fury. "Pardon me?"

"Give it a break, *Jake*. I don't know how you fooled her into believing you're Evan, but the game's up. You'd better tell me it hasn't gone further than what I saw tonight, or I'm going to have to rip your heart out with my bare hands." Her fingers turned into claws in readiness for the attack.

"Settle down, Chloe. She knows I'm not Evan."

"She *knows*? Oh, come on. I've seen the gags you've pulled on her and I know how crazy you get when she's around, but I never thought you'd stoop this low."

"If I *had* stooped that low, do you really think she wouldn't have noticed the difference?"

She stared at him, nonplussed. "*I* sure as hell did. The first kiss you laid on her had me suspicious, but I chalked it up to the surprise of the party. By the time you got around to that last kiss...ha!...you and Evan aren't even in the same species."

"Which species seems to make her happier?" It wasn't a rhetorical question. He sincerely wanted to know.

"For heaven's sake," cried Chloe, shaking her head incredulously, "you're not only unscrupulous, you're delusional. You don't really think that your masquerade can possibly make her *happy!* She'll be humiliated. Devastated. Don't fool yourself, Jake—if she knew who you were, she wouldn't spit on you to put out a fire."

"Your eloquence moves me to tears, Chloe," he uttered with a wry twist of his mouth, "but as unlikely as it seems, she knows who I am."

She gawked at him, visibly making the effort to give his story a fair shake. "Then why is she letting you kiss her?"

"I don't know." And he realized it was true. He hadn't the slightest idea why Brianna was letting him kiss her.

All too quickly, he remembered why. He was supposed to be helping her overcome inhibitions. How could he have forgotten that? *Because you wanted to.*

"If she knows who you are," challenged Chloe, "then why is she pretending you're Evan?"

Jake closed his eyes and rubbed his hand across his eyelids and the bridge of his nose. He'd obviously made a big mistake in coming here tonight. Even so, nothing could have kept him away. "Call her in and we'll talk about it."

"Don't worry, I plan to." She paced to the door. "I'm warning you, Jake. If we're springing some surprise on Brianna, you will *not* leave this room alive."

"I CAN'T BELIEVE you didn't trust me enough to clue me in."

"It wasn't my secret to tell, Chloe," Brianna countered. "I gave my word to Cy Rowland, and if you hadn't guessed the truth I never would have broken that word."

"Okay, okay, I know how you are about keeping promises."

Brianna sat on the bed watching as Chloe paced. She'd sent Jake from the room shortly after they'd explained the fundamentals of the situation.

"You've explained why Jake's pretending to be Evan," Chloe said, "but not why you're so lovey-dovey with Jake. You looked like a couple on their honeymoon, hardly able to wait to get back to—" Her eyes widened and her jaw dropped. "Don't tell me you went to bed with *him!*"

Brianna raised her chin, determined to remain in control of her emotions, which seemed stretched to their limits. "I appreciate your concern, but—"

"I'm worried about you, Bri! You told me you were in love with Evan. Now you're going to bed with Jake?"

"Evan and I broke up," she imparted, glad to be able finally to admit it. "He sent me a letter saying he wants to be 'just friends.'"

"Oh, Bri, I'm sorry. I should have known you wouldn't go to bed with Jake if you were still involved with Evan." Chloe shook her head. "That explains a lot. You were in a highly vulnerable state. You went to Jake on the rebound. At least you're getting over your hang-up about sex, I guess. Too bad it's with the wrong guy."

A surprising pain pierced Brianna. As much as she wanted to tell Chloe she was wrong, she couldn't. Jake *was* the wrong guy. The very worst guy in the world for her. Any other man she'd be able to leave—or rather, shove out the door—the moment the relationship grew uncomfortable. She couldn't do that with Jake. He wielded some strong, uncanny power over her that kept her with him, even while her head begged her to put an end to their affair.

Then again, why should she worry about ending their affair? He'd be leaving her as soon as Evan returned. Their affair would die a natural death. She felt as if her heart might die along with it.

"Bri, I'm sorry." Chloe sat on the bed and slipped an arm around her. "I shouldn't have said that. I can't think of anyone better qualified to help you learn to enjoy sex than a stud like Jake."

Brianna's breath caught. "Don't call him that." She hadn't meant to sound so sharp, but something inside her couldn't allow anyone to talk that way about him.

Chloe's lips slowly parted and her hand rose to her cheek. "Oh, no. Oh, no!" In horror, she cried, "You're falling in love with him, aren't you?"

"Don't even say that!" This time the rebuke rang out with deliberate sharpness. "I'm *not* in love with Jake, and I never will be."

"I hope not. I really hope not." Her usually sparkling eyes now shone with worry. "I mean, he's a lot of fun, but you can't get caught up in the game. Face it, Bri— you're a hometown porch-swing kind of girl. A guy like Jake would gobble you up, just for the novelty of it, then fly off in his private Learjet."

Unable to utter a rational reply, Brianna bent her head and made for the door. Swinging it open, she stopped short.

There stood Jake, leaning in a negligent pose with one hand against the wall, the other hooked in his hip pocket. His solemn stare held her arrested, then flickered beyond her. "You really should be aware, Chloe, that voices carry pretty far from your bedroom."

He then turned his dark, unsmiling eyes to Brianna. "Let's go, Bri," he whispered. "Wouldn't want to let my private Learjet sit idle for too long."

HE WAS DAMNED GLAD she'd come with him. For a moment he'd thought she wouldn't, and drastic impulses shot through his mind, most involving physical abduction. He wouldn't have left without her.

He escorted Brianna into the clear, frigid November night, down the driveway to where the Mercedes was parked. Only the crunching of snow beneath their feet disturbed their silence. As he opened her car door, the conversation he'd overheard returned to him in disturbing flashes.

Brianna had come to him in a "highly vulnerable state," Chloe had said. "On the rebound." He supposed that should make him feel guilty. It didn't. If she had to be vulnerable to let him inside her defensive walls, so be it.

Chloe had also called him "the wrong guy." His teeth gritted at that. She'd meant that Evan was the right guy. Brianna hadn't argued. *I'm not in love with Jake*, she'd said, *and I never will be*.

He slammed the car door and buried his hands in his coat pockets as he strode to the driver's side. The problem was, *he* loved *her*—so much that he didn't know how he'd ever "keep it light." But he had to. Love was a tricky, treacherous thing that he never had understood. All he knew was that a wrong move, a wrong word could snatch a person he loved out of his reach.

Neither of them spoke as they drove down a rural

highway toward her house; the silence between them was uncomfortable.

"Jake," she finally said as they reached a backstreet of town, her tone a pitiful attempt at lightness, "Despite everything, I...I enjoyed being with you at the party."

"Yeah, I'm a real fun guy."

She pressed her lips together and looked down at her lap. As he parked the car in front of her house, she murmured, "If Chloe and I said something in that conversation that hurt your feelings or insulted you, I'm...I'm sorry."

"I can't imagine what *that* would have been." He lifted a quizzical brow at her. "Did you think I'd take it as an insult that Chloe called me a stud?" She didn't answer, but he sensed her discomfort and in a near whisper demanded, "Why did you stop her from saying it?"

She lifted her palms, at a loss for an answer.

"You know what a stud is, don't you?" he persisted. "It's a male used for sex."

She made an inarticulate sound in her throat.

"What's the matter, Brianna?" His voice had grown gruff, and he couldn't gentle it. "Does that hit a little too close to home?"

"If you're talking about you and me," she cried in choked tones, "then I don't need your...your stud service." She made a move toward the door handle.

He caught her arms and held her still, searching her face. "I'm not the one who ever thought of us that way. This sex thing we have going is a two-way deal. I'm there for you and you're there for me."

A sheen welled in her eyes. "That's not a very big difference."

"It is to me," he whispered. Slipping his fingers into her luxuriant hair, he caressed her face with his own, his eyes tightly closed. "I need you tonight, Brianna. And tomorrow, and the day after that."

"Oh, Jake." Her head lolled back against the leather seat as he kissed her throat. "What are we doing?"

"Whatever it is, we've already started...and we can't stop in the middle." He dissolved her doubts with hot, determined kisses.

He didn't understand love, but he understood sex. He knew how to play music within her, when others apparently hadn't even struck a chord. That had to mean something. He'd use that "something" to bind her to him...until she needed him the way she needed food or air or water.

The way he needed her.

11

A COUPLE ON THEIR honeymoon. Chloe's description drifted back to Brianna as she sat at her desk Monday morning. It had been a strikingly apt description of how Jake and she had spent the remainder of the weekend— making love, sometimes with a passionate urgency, sometimes with sweet, erotic tenderness that filled her to overflowing.

If only their time together didn't have to end. It would soon, though. Jake had received a call from a detective he'd hired. The embezzler had been traced. He had her under surveillance, hoping to find the stolen money.

"Have the police take her in," Jake had instructed. "Let them know that if she doesn't sign a confession and return the cash, we're going to spend twice that much to convict her and keep her in prison."

Evan, it seemed, would be coming home very soon. As relieved as Brianna was to know that his nightmare would be over, she didn't want to think about Jake leaving. She wanted so much to live on in the day-to-day relationship they'd forged. To keep on loving him.

She stiffened. Is that what she was doing? *Loving* him?

A sharp rapping at her office door distracted her from that alarming thought. She opened the door and Maude rushed in, her thin, weathered face pasty white. "I have to talk to you, Ms. Devon. I think something terrible is happening."

She took the secretary's cold, rigid hands and guided her to the sofa. "Sit down, Maude, and tell me what's wrong."

"Maybe I should have told you sooner, but Cy Rowland called me last week and asked me to spy on Jake."

"To spy on Jake!"

"He told me to make copies of all his paperwork and computer disks. It seems he doesn't trust him."

"But Cy was the one who put him in charge!"

"Only to stand in for Evan. He didn't mean for him to start fooling around with the company. At least, that's what Cy's secretary told me."

Brianna stared at Maude in mute disbelief. Jake had told her he had the authorization he needed to make those changes. Had he lied to her? Had he been acting without Cy's approval? "Why would Jake make changes that Cy or Evan would overrule? It's only a matter of time before Evan returns."

"Cy believes that Jake sees this as a game, and that he's trying to outdo Evan. Maybe even wrest the power away from him. Corporate one-upmanship."

Brianna refused to believe it. Surely Jake cared more about the company—and his brother—than that! *Think back*, an inner voice scoffed. *You'd have easily believed it before your affair with him. Have you become blinded to his true character?* Her mother had been blinded by a man, too— a man she thought loved her—until she'd lost everything.

"Do you know Jake has made inquiries into selling the executive golf course and the new expansion building?" Maude disclosed.

"No, he never said a word about those."

"I did a little research into his business background.

He owns a company called Global Corporate Consultants."

Brianna didn't find that as surprising as she once would have. Jake was no stranger to corporate business. He'd tried to tell her during Cy's meeting, she remembered; he'd claimed to have worked as a corporate consultant. She hadn't believed him then. She hadn't yet seen him in action.

"Do you know what his company does, Ms. Devon?" In a black whisper, she revealed, "They *downsize* corporations."

"Downsize!" repeated Brianna, aghast.

"He's known as a hatchet man. He chops workers out of jobs. Terminates their positions. He'd be a hero in the stockholders' eyes if he downsized our staff, cut the overhead and upped their stock value. But workers would be laid off after years of loyal service."

"He can't do that without the approval of the board."

"He's selling off company assets, isn't he?"

"I'm sure he'll have to present every sale to the board for their final okay."

"It's a family business, Ms. Devon, and we don't know if stock has changed hands among the family members. Jake may have acquired a voting majority. Nor do we know what tricks he has up his sleeve. I've read about corporate maneuvers involving stocks and takeovers and things I don't understand. I'll bet Jake understands them."

An ache formed in Brianna's heart. "Oh, Maude, we can't jump to conclusions. Where is Jake?"

"I don't know. That's one of the reasons I decided to talk to you about this. Something big is going on right now. Jake was working on his computer, then jumped up and yelled at me to get Evan on the line. Meanwhile,

Cy called, demanding to talk to Jake. Then Jake told me to cancel all his appointments and raced out of here like he was on fire.''

Forcing herself to maintain her composure, Brianna assured Maude that she'd done the right thing in telling her. After the secretary had returned to her desk, Brianna dialed Jake's cell phone. His line was busy.

Had he been operating with some hidden agenda? No, there had to be another explanation for Cy's spying. She needed badly to hear it.

ALONE IN THE HOSPITAL waiting room, Jake hung up from his call to Evan's stockbroker and glanced at his watch. Cy had been in with a doctor for nearly an hour. They'd either sedated him or promised to send him home; Jake no longer heard him yelling. An ambulance had rushed him in for chest pains—a possible heart attack—but Jake knew that nothing would keep Cy Rowland in the hospital now.

Not while his favorite company in the conglomerate was collapsing under its own weight. And that's just what was happening with the Rowland Insurance Company.

Evan's high-risk investments had bottomed out.

Jake curled his lip in dour reflection. He hadn't wanted the old man to learn about the plummeting stocks until he'd come up with a plan of action to soften the blow. Evan's investments had been a private transaction, not listed in the corporate minutes. Cy wouldn't have known about the investments if it hadn't been for his spying.

He'd had Maude making copies of his paperwork and reporting on his every move, as he'd told Jake this morning. Too bad the old codger hadn't done the same while

Evan had been running the company. He could have stopped him from making those risky investments in the first place.

The company's downfall now seemed imminent. The investment failure was the proverbial straw that would break the camel's back. After Evan's mismanagement, the company was too weak to survive it. Too many assets would have to be liquidated to cover the loss.

"Mr. Rowland?" A bearded doctor approached and shook hands with Jake. "We're keeping your grandfather for a few more hours. If he remains stable, he'll be free to go home."

Jake gave the doctor his cell phone number, then strode out of the hospital and into the bright November day. He felt the need to walk, far and long. As he headed for the wooded towpath that ran between the old canal and the river, his cell phone rang. He tensed, bracing himself for whatever news it might bring.

Brianna's voice rushed over him like a soothing balm. "Maude said you left in a hurry. Is something wrong?"

"Cy had a few chest pains. He's doing okay now."

"Thank goodness for that. I...I need to talk to you." Her voice sounded strained, and he wondered if she'd already heard about the plummeting stocks.

"Come meet me." He wanted to see her, needed the comfort of her presence. He'd have to break the news of the company's downfall to her, but he wasn't ready to talk about it yet. How could he explain without mentioning Evan's mistakes? He'd promised Evan not to tell her. He couldn't betray his brother's trust, especially not when his life was caving in on him. From the reedy pitch of Evan's voice this morning, Jake knew he couldn't handle more stress right now.

"Where should I meet you?" Brianna asked.

"The towpath. Remember the place where I chained your tenth-grade boyfriend's bike to the bench?"

"Yeah, I remember."

"Meet me there."

WITH HER THROAT clogged by too many burning questions, Brianna trod along the wide leaf-strewn towpath of the Ohio & Erie trail, where horses had once pulled barges down the lazy-moving canal.

She found Jake not on the wrought iron bench, as she'd expected, but on the bridge beyond it, leaning against its wooden rail, gazing across the green, rushing river that ran parallel to the canal. His dark brown hair glinted golden in the sunlight and rippled in the breeze. The masculine beauty of his strong, lean face and sturdy form struck her once again and deepened the ache inside her.

She couldn't bear to think that he might be playing some game that could affect her company, her community, her future. *But what if he was?* Fighting to keep her voice level, she called out, "Is your grandfather all right?"

He turned toward her, and she noticed a disturbing soberness in his expression. "I'm sure he will be. He's too ornery to stay down long. Let's walk." He held his hand out for her, and her heart begged her to take it.

But she couldn't. She hung back, wrapping her arms around herself and shivering in the November chill. "Were you telling me the truth, Jake, when you said you had Cy's approval to make changes?"

Dismay was reflected in his gaze, and he lowered his outstretched hand. "That's not what I told you. I said I had all the authorization I needed."

"What's the difference?"

"I didn't bring Cy into it. He's not strong enough, healthwise, to deal with the pressure. But I *am* acting within the authorization granted to the company's CEO."

"Evan's the real CEO."

"The board granted me legal authorization for as long as I'm doing his job. It was the only way I agreed to do it."

Realization clutched at her. "You lied to me, Jake! You let me think you had Cy's approval. If I'd known the truth, I wouldn't have helped you."

"No?" Although his voice remained soft, a steeliness entered his eyes, turning them more gray than blue. "Would you have spied on me like Maude did, if he'd asked you?"

She didn't know. *Would* she have spied for Cy? The company had to be her top priority, and Cy was its ultimate authority. But even now, she found herself unwilling to doubt Jake's integrity. "I would have confronted you, like I'm doing now. So answer my questions, damn you. What are you doing? Why are you selling company assets?"

"Our cash reserve is too low to cover potential losses."

"Did the embezzlement affect us *that badly?*" she cried, incredulous that it could.

He remained silent too long. "It didn't help."

There was something he wasn't telling her. She knew him well enough to be sure of that. "Is it true," she whispered, "that you're called a hatchet man?"

A muscle moved in his jaw. "I might have been called that at times by resentful employees."

"So you *do* specialize in downsizing companies?"

"No, I specialize in saving them."

"Are you planning to downsize Rowland Insurance?"

A harshness invaded his whisper. "Downsizing wouldn't be so bad."

She released her breath in a rush. He intended to cut workers out of their jobs! Blade-sharp pain sliced through her. "To you, a cut in our workforce might be just another way to increase the bottom line, but to our workers, it's the end of their livelihood."

"Downsizing sometimes keeps a company solvent."

"I can't believe that's the case here!"

"You're right. It's not."

She heard his denial, but no reassurance. A premonition of disaster prickled up her spine. "Then what is the case?"

"Downsizing won't help now." His voice had grown gruff, almost raw. "If you want answers, walk with me. I've got to walk." He strode across the bridge and down the towpath.

Anxiety clawed at her as she followed him. She expected him to talk, to offer explanations, but moments passed and not a word was spoken.

"You understand how important this company is to Pleasantville, don't you, Jake?" she said, frightened now. She had no idea what kind of game he was playing, but she sensed it had gotten out of control. "This town couldn't exist without it. People would have to move to find jobs. We're surrounded by Amish farmland, in case you've forgotten."

"I realize that, Brianna."

"Without Rowland Insurance, the small businesses would fold. The whole town would fold. Look at this canal." She flung a hand toward the gentle current on their left. "It used to be the lifeblood of this place. When the canals closed down, the town died. Fifty years went by before Rowland Insurance brought it back to life. It could die again, Jake. We have to keep the company strong."

He came to a sudden halt and frowned down at her with an intensity that scared her. "Some things I can't control. The company has hit bad times."

"How...how bad?" she whispered.

"Investments took a plunge. We may not recover."

Her mouth moved, but no sounds came out. Jake had no problem reading her eyes, though. She looked as if he'd stabbed her. Her anguish twisted like a knife in his gut.

"I won't let things get bad for you, Brianna. You can come on the road with me. You're good with people. I've got a heavy schedule and I can use your help."

Her eyes widened as if he'd suggested she murder someone for pay.

"I'll hire you at double your present salary," he said, realizing how perfect a solution it would be to the dilemma of leaving her. That prospect had been eating a hole in him for too long now. "You can have any title you want."

Her lips grew thin; her eyes blazed some vehement message. She whirled and stalked away. A terrible coldness gripped him. Life would be too empty without her.

As she reached the bridge, she stopped, and hope reared up within him. "I want to talk to Evan."

Evan. Of course. How could he have forgotten? Reality splashed over him like icy water, dousing his hope. She would never come on the road with him and leave Evan behind.

Tonelessly he replied, "I'll have him call you."

She resumed walking.

THE NEWS HAD hit her so hard that she felt dazed and sickened. The company was going under—the only company she'd ever worked for. The town would fold, she'd lose her house and probably have to move away to find a job.

Hurting her just as badly was the fact that Jake had betrayed her. All the while they'd been playing their sex games, he'd apparently been playing secret corporate games, as well. She'd been right all those years to run from him. When she'd finally stopped running, he'd distracted her from the important things, and now she'd lost everything.

And he planned to hop on his private jet and move on to the next game. Oh, he'd been generous enough to offer her a ride. How long would it have taken him to want a new playmate? He simply had no understanding of serious commitments—to a town, a company, a family or an individual. Nothing meant much to Jake. And nothing had ever hurt her more than that fact.

Operating by rote, she returned to work. Maude followed her into her office. "Cy's secretary said he had a heart attack over the things Jake did," Maude proclaimed, her eyes red and swollen. "He made high-risk investments, Ms. Devon, and now we might go under!"

Fighting against her own barely repressed panic Brianna choked out some vague nonsense about not giving up hope, then she locked her office door. A garbled version of the truth would surely get around, and employees would come to her with questions. She was in no condition to answer.

She could do little more than contemplate the enormity of the blow that had struck them all. Beneath the anger, the fear and the intense pain loomed a deep bewilderment. How could a healthy company be destroyed by an embezzlement or even a few bad investments? If the company had been strong, those things should have meant little more than setbacks. The risks Jake took must have been huge.

She found it so hard to believe of the Jake she'd come to know. But he *had* been hiding something from her when she'd asked what had caused the company's downfall.

Evan's call came quickly. At least Jake had kept his word about that. She supposed she should be grateful.

"Evan, are things as bad with the company as Jake says? He told me we might not be able to recover after the embezzlement and some investment failure."

"It might be true." He sounded weak and wretched; nothing like the professional, confident man she'd known.

"But we were a strong, growing company before the embezzlement. Either a tremendous amount of money was stolen or Jake must have taken huge risks to land us in this mess. Which one was it?"

"I...I don't know exactly *what* happened, Brianna." An anguished silence fell. "We'll figure it out when I get home. But don't blame Jake. He's doing the best he can."

Disappointment robbed her of a reply. She'd been hoping for an explanation that would exonerate Jake. There obviously wasn't one.

"Jake hasn't been bothering you, has he?" Evan asked.

"Bothering me?" *You mean other than ruining my life?*

"Asking you out." Evan sounded somewhat embarrassed. "You know...coming on to you."

What, she wondered, had Jake told him?

"The only reason I ask," he continued, "is that he said he intended to. Since we broke up, he considers you fair game. I know you've never liked him much, but he can be persuasive. He wouldn't hurt you deliberately, but...well, you're not like the fast women he's used to."

No, I'm much more stupid. She felt as if she'd been punched in the stomach for the umpteenth time that day.

"Brianna, I...I miss you."

"We'll talk when you get home."

After quiet goodbyes, she sat staring into space. Jake had called her fair game. Fair game! And she'd been too wrapped up in their affair to even realize he was playing. Prince Charming had swept her off her feet. Now the ball had ended, and he'd dumped her into the ashes.

Anger, hot and reviving, buoyed her head above the panic and the pain, at least enough for her to breathe. She had to keep a watch out for Prince Charming's return. She intended to turn his pleasure ride back into rats and pumpkins.

Around three o'clock that afternoon, Jake strode into his office, looking somber. Before he'd had a chance to take off his coat, Brianna flung open their adjoining door.

"I'm taking my work home with me, Jake. And I won't be back until Evan's sitting behind that desk. Maybe he'll find a way to clean up the mess you've made of this company."

"The mess *I've* made?" A frown darkened his face. "Did you talk to Evan?"

"Yes, and he defended you, as usual. Too bad you don't care as much about him. His business and reputation are the most important things in his life, yet you played around with the company and took some huge gamble with our funds."

"Do you really think I'd risk your future, my brother's and the town's, just for *kicks?*" His anger shook some of the certainty right out of her. "If you think that, why the hell did you have anything to do with me? What were all those long, hot kisses about, and the hours we spent in bed?"

"We both know the answer to that one—*sex*. A convenience for us both during your impersonation. After all, I was fair game, wasn't I?"

She'd taken him by surprise. Dismay flickered through his anger. She realized then that she'd been clinging to some pitiful hope that he'd deny it. In a pained whisper, she confirmed, "You called me that, didn't you?"

He shut his eyes in a brief wince. "Yes, but I—"

"Game over." With her heart breaking, she turned toward the door.

He stepped in her way. "I didn't play with company funds, Brianna, and I never considered you any kind of game. For once in your life, give me the benefit of the doubt. Believe in me."

There, in the heat of his imploring stare, she realized the very worst had happened. She had fallen in love with him. Terribly in love. She had every reason to believe that he'd torn apart her world, yet she wanted to trust him. His dark, uncanny power had finally invaded the part of her she'd guarded the most—her reasoning.

Propelled by a heart-pounding fear, she shoved past him. On her way out the door, she uttered, "Stay away from me, Jake. I don't ever want to see you again."

THE DAYS THAT followed were pure agony. Brianna refused to return to the office while Jake was in charge. She couldn't bear to see him, hear him or even hear about him. She'd forwarded her office phone to her home, but most of the calls were from employees asking questions about rumors that had been circulating. Brianna relied on her answering machine to screen the calls.

One asked if Jake Rowland had been impersonating Evan. Another wanted to know if Jake had been sent to downsize the company or if he intended to take it over. Others asked if they should start looking for jobs, and one message even included the phrase, "hatchet man."

Although Maude had undoubtedly shared her suspicions about Jake and unwittingly started the rumors, she hadn't gone so far as to mention the company's probable downfall. Her faith in Evan wouldn't allow that. "When he comes back, he'll find a way to save the company," she'd told Brianna.

The employees, therefore, suspected only a downsizing, and their image of Jake as an invading corporate shark continued to feed their distrust. Brianna didn't know how anyone, even someone as insensitive as Jake, could face down all that animosity. And yet, he had. Two days after she'd walked out on him, her secretary called with the day's news.

He'd held another meeting. The mood of his audience this time had been cold and suspicious, yet he'd stood before them and admitted the company was having problems.

"You should have heard all the muttering," Theresa said. "Someone yelled 'hatchet man,' and Ellie stood up and asked if he was really Jake instead of Evan. He politely asked her to sit down, then finished saying what he had to say."

"Which was...?" Brianna had prompted.

"That as soon as he knew more, he'd tell us. Until then, we're to do our jobs as if the company depended on it. Then he left. I haven't seen him back in the office since."

He'd left? *For good?*

Ridiculous though it was, anguish hit Brianna anew. She couldn't help wondering where he'd gone, what he was doing, and how he felt about the company's crisis. She thought of their personal times, the laughs they'd shared, the tender, passionate lovemaking. The way he'd kissed her as if his heart and soul had joined with hers.

As she analyzed the depth of her heartache, she realized that she'd begun to believe he'd fallen in love with her. And she missed him with an almost unbearable ache.

But his recklessness had hurt her and their hometown. She couldn't fall into the trap her mother had—forgiving a lover, only to be hurt again, until her spirit was broken. She'd allow no one to break her spirit. She was stronger than that. Lonely, yes. Maybe even heartbroken, but still master of her own destiny.

What destiny? She, who had lived to build a secure future, could now plan for nothing, depend on nothing. Her job would end, her savings would dwindle, her house would sell for little or nothing. She'd be living somewhere among strangers, lucky to find a job making half of what she earned now.

The day she'd always dreaded had arrived. She'd lost everything—her job, her home, her heart. She had nothing and no one to depend on...except herself. At her bleakest hour in the loneliest night, a realization hit her. It was enough. She could still depend on herself!

She might be left heartbroken and with no assets to her name, but she still had her degree, nine years of solid work experience with good references and a strong credit history. She knew how to make friends and how to care about people. As much as she'd miss her present life, she would survive.

It was a dazzling revelation. Her fear of this very predicament had ruled her for too long. She'd been ready to live without love—passionate, fulfilling love—because she'd been afraid of losing her self-reliance.

She had loved. And she had lost. But she hadn't lost herself. In fact, she'd grown.

Love made the spirit stronger, she realized, and more able to face adversity. That was the difference between love and the sick dependence her mother had mistaken for the real thing.

Brianna switched on her bedside lamp and lay against her pillows, marveling. She could let herself love.

But a different bleakness soon filled her, and this one hurt more than the fear itself had. Jake was the man who made both her body and soul come alive, and he didn't understand a thing about love—even with his own family.

He didn't understand that love meant sticking around after the fun wore thin and the hard times hit. He didn't understand that love meant shouldering the burden when it grew heavy. He didn't understand feeling your loved ones' pain and doing everything possible to ease it.

A memory flashed like lightning through her, a small detail that had almost escaped her notice: the emotion in Jake's eyes the last time she'd seen him. It had looked very much like pain.

It might have been regret. Or guilt, or the smarting of a bruised ego. More than likely, it had been the agony of defeat. He had, after all, lost at a high-stakes game. He

would have to deal with those feelings on his own. He'd
brought them on with his own reckless actions.

She told herself to forget him. He didn't know how to
love, and he certainly didn't love her. She'd merely been
fair game.

But she couldn't forget him...or the pain she'd seen so
briefly in his eyes.

12

"GOOD MORNING, Ms. Devon," Maude greeted over the phone. "Cy Rowland is expecting you to attend a meeting this morning." With a note of pique in her voice, she added, "*I* wasn't invited."

Brianna sat on her bed with the phone wedged against her shoulder as she finished pinning a colorful scarf against her tailored gray suit. She hoped it might help her inject a dash of optimism into the day, which she'd planned to spend at the office. "Where will the meeting be held?"

"Cy's house, since he hasn't fully recovered yet."

Despite her newly found determination to make the best of a bad situation, her anxiety rose. Would Jake be there? "Did his secretary say who else will be attending?"

"Board members and the Rowland family. Evan will be flying in this morning from France. The embezzler was arrested, and charges against Evan have been dropped."

"Thank heavens." She wondered if Jake would return with him. "Will anyone else be at the meeting?" she prodded.

"If you mean Jake Rowland, I wouldn't know." Maude gave a vexed sniff. "From what I've heard about him, he's probably sunning himself in the Caribbean by now."

Maude's scorn bothered her. As angry as Brianna herself had been with Jake, she didn't like to hear others peck at him. She hadn't been able to forget that flash of pain in his eyes. She wanted so much for a chance to take a closer look.

As she began her trek to Cy's house, she noticed her co-workers walking in the same direction. Why? The meeting wouldn't include the general employee population.

Climbing the steep driveway edged with well-trimmed evergreens, she encountered more employees. No one seemed anxious to talk to her. At the top of the circular drive, a crowd of them gathered on the massive front lawn below the white-columned portico.

She guessed, then, why they had assembled. They'd heard about the board meeting and knew of its importance. They'd probably also heard of Evan's scheduled return, although word hadn't yet leaked out about the embezzlement that had kept him overseas. She couldn't blame them for wanting definite answers about their future.

She nodded to her peers, and whispers carried to her.

"Could she have been fooled, too?"

"No, she was friends with 'em both..."

"I heard that Jake moved her office next to his so she could help him take the company apart...."

Keeping her gaze straight ahead, she climbed the front stairway, reeling from the unexpected blows. She loved these people. She'd give anything to prevent their loss. How could they think she'd betray them? But then, how could they not? She'd been with Jake the entire time. She'd pulled files for him, shared stories about each employee, listened in on many of his meetings.

She knew he hadn't set out to downsize the company,

as the employees believed. The changes he'd made had all been sound. Why, then, had he invested so much of their cash in high-risk stocks? Hadn't he known better? The chronic ache that had become an integral part of her suddenly began to throb. *Give me the benefit of the doubt,* he'd implored.

What if he'd truly believed he was helping the company? The pain she'd seen might have been the same one she felt now. Although her co-workers believed the worst about her, her intentions had been good. Had Jake been trying his best, as Evan had claimed on the phone?

As she reached the wide columned veranda, she heard a murmur rustle through the crowd. She turned to see a car gliding around the curve of the circular drive. Evan's Mercedes. It parked between a Rolls-Royce and Bentley.

The Rowland twins got out. Both of them.

Brianna felt a squeezing around her heart. Both were clean shaven, with deep tans, neatly cropped hair and expensive suits. Their handsome features were, of course, identical. This time, though, she had no problem telling the brothers apart.

Evan paused near the passenger door and gazed at the crowd, which had gone stone silent. He forced a smile, but his eyes retained a furtive look—as if he wanted only to dash past the gathering to the sanctuary of the house.

Jake shut the driver's door and sauntered toward the stairway, his gaze wandering casually over the crowd. Evan followed him. All eyes swung from one twin to the other. Brianna realized that no one else could tell them apart.

"Welcome back, Evan!" a man yelled.

Another voice piped up, "Where you been?"

"Straighten out the mess, Ev!"

"Keep us working!"

"Go sun yourself, Jake!"

"Chop up some other company, hatchet man...!"

The yells fused into a roar.

Evan kept his eyes straight ahead as he walked. Brianna herself had reacted in the same way to the crowd's hostility. But that hostility wasn't directed at Evan—only at Jake and her. As Evan drew nearer, she saw the germ of panic in his face. What had all this stress done to him?

Jake strolled up the steps looking entirely unaffected. His gaze settled on Brianna. His lips tightened almost imperceptibly and he looked away from her toward Evan as he climbed the stairs. When he'd reached the top, Jake uttered, "Go inside." Neither Evan nor Brianna complied.

Jake turned and faced the angry crowd. With calm authority, he held out his hands and quieted them. From the doubtful looks on the upturned faces, Brianna knew that the crowd still hadn't decided which Rowland twin addressed them.

"Thank you for your support," Jake began. "You've been good, loyal workers." The hostility left their gazes. They thought he was Evan. "As much as I want to, I can't promise everything's going to turn out okay. We'll do what we can to keep you working." Applause broke out, even as worry furrowed most brows. "Go back to your jobs. Man the front lines. Let's not fall apart under pressure."

The crowd slowly dispersed, calling out encouragements. Jake nodded in acknowledgment. When the last of the workers had left, he followed his brother and Brianna into the house.

Admiration for him revived all the warmer feelings that she'd tried so hard to quell. He'd handled a predicament that had been too emotionally charged for his brother to face. She sensed a terrible tension in Evan, as if he'd snap in two at any moment. When Jake had closed the door, she turned to Evan in grave concern. He seemed too choked up to speak. Instead, he hugged her.

Jake strode past them without a glance.

They followed him through high-ceilinged rooms where their footsteps echoed on marble floors, then down long carpeted corridors. Brianna remembered whispering with Evan long ago in this hallowed wing occupied by Cy.

They rounded a corner and a woman's joyous cry stopped them. "Mister Jake!" A plump grizzle-haired woman in a dark dress and white apron rushed to him with arms outspread. "I didn't think you'd ever come back to this house again!"

Jake caught her in a hug. "I came to get *you*, Lucy. You ready to run away with me yet?"

She laughed with boisterous delight. "You'll never be good 'nough for me, I tol' you that. I'm wearing that watch you sent me, though. See?" She held up her wrist.

"I didn't send you a watch."

"Don't you lie! Who else sends me presents from Germany or Switzerland or whichever place this one's from?"

"Had to be that rich boyfriend of yours."

Cackling, she shook her graying head. "You gonna be here Sunday? I'm making my fried chicken."

"No, I'll be leaving before then." With a peculiar dryness, he added, "My, uh, private Learjet's ready to go." Although he hadn't glanced her way, Brianna knew the remark had been aimed at her. His subtle yet sharp-edged sarcasm hurt—as did the fact that he'd be leaving so soon.

Lucy muttered in disapproval and toddled past him. "Mr. Evan, 'bout time you're home." She enfolded him in a warm embrace. "Now you boys behave when you go in with Mister Cy. Don't get him too upset. All them old uncles and cousins he calls the 'board' are in with him now."

Jake sent Evan a speaking glance. *You ready for this?* Evan drew in an unsteady breath. Apprehension zipped through Brianna as Jake led them to Cy's bedroom.

They heard his low growl through an open door. "It was sibling rivalry, I say. He wanted to prove himself better at business, even if he had to take asinine risks to do it."

"I believe you're right, Cy," replied a deeper, slower voice. "I heard those boys even went after the same gal."

"Oh, hush, Henry," warbled a woman, "that's nothing but gossip. I heard she's just an old friend of theirs."

Brianna froze in the corridor outside Cy's room. They were talking about her. *Had* Jake been using her to compete with Evan? He'd known they were having problems—sexual problems. Had he set out to prove himself the better lover?

Her gaze locked with Jake's. His jaw tightened and a message blazed clearly in his cobalt eyes. *Believe in me.*

And she realized that she did. She knew, as surely as the sun rises, that their lovemaking had meant more to him than that. Much more. She turned away to hide the question that hammered through her veins. What exactly *had* their lovemaking meant?

When she'd regained a clear focus, she saw Evan staring at Jake as if he'd realized some basic truth. She squeezed Evan's arm in a silent plea to ignore the hurtful rumor.

At her gesture, Jake looked away, pushed open the door and strode inside. Evan motioned for Brianna to go in ahead of him. Gathering her dignity, she made a quiet entrance.

In a vast, plush bedchamber decorated in muted shades of blue, Cy peered at them from the pillows of a stately bed, his hair an unruly shock of white and his droopy eyes grim. "Come in. Sit down."

The other elderly ladies and gentleman, all dressed for business, nodded briefly from wing-backed armchairs on the far side of the bed. Jake settled into the chair closest to Cy. Brianna sank down into the one beside Jake, with Evan on her other side. The air felt close and explosive.

"I want to start by apologizing," rumbled Cy, his voice solemn and hoarse. "I shouldn't have allowed my grandson free rein. I've always known how competitive he is. It's an obsession with him, to prove that he's the best."

She sensed Jake stiffen in the chair beside her. She wished she could spare him this ordeal.

Cy obviously didn't share her compassion. "Knowing that he could lose it all, he gambled away the company's funds." His voice picked up volume. "It was more important to him to prove himself brilliant than to insure long-term stability."

Brianna resorted to teeth grinding. No matter what mistakes Jake might have made, his grandfather had no right to humiliate him like this.

"He didn't understand the fundamentals of growth or diversification," railed Cy. "And I'm just as much to blame for granting him too much power—giving him

the rope to hang himself on those stupid, careless investments."

Brianna couldn't hold back any longer. "Mistakes
might have been made," she called out, startling Cy,
"but they couldn't have been stupid or careless. If
there's one thing I've learned about your grandson, it's
the fact that he is extremely skilled and conscientious in
business. Whatever gambles he took, he believed them
to be for the best."

Cy frowned, taken aback. Jake scrutinized her intently.

She lifted her chin and pressed on. "He did a lot of
good things for the company. He brightened morale,
opened lines of communication and initiated *wonderful*
programs."

"Ms. Devon, he ran the company to the ground! I've
heard you have a close personal relationship with him,
but it's time you took off your rose-colored glasses."

"My close personal relationship with him has nothing
to do with it," she exclaimed, flushed and earnest. "I
find it hard to believe that a few bad investments or even
an embezzlement could ruin a healthy company. There's
more going on here than meets the eye." She stood up,
her jaw squared. "Fire me, if you'd like. Terminate me
without references. But I won't sit here and listen to you
and everyone else blame the company's downfall on
Jake!"

The silence quivered around them like shock waves.
Everyone gaped at her as if she'd lost her mind. Jake
himself stared, looking thunderstruck. The only thing
moving in the room was Evan's mouth. It opened and
closed in what appeared to be a futile attempt to speak.

Cy's bushy white brows bunched. "Did you
say...*Jake?*"

Unsure of the point behind his question, she nodded.

"Brianna," Evan interjected, finally finding his voice, "he wasn't talking about Jake. He was talking about me."

She blinked a few times rapidly to clear her vision, to comprehend his words, to make sense of the situation....

"*I* made the bad investments," Evan clarified. "And you're right. The company wasn't in good shape when Jake took over. I just wanted to *grow.* I wanted to bring in major accounts, but once I did I had to scramble to plug up holes in the reserve. I took the risk with the funds because my back was against the wall. And then—" he grimaced "—the embezzlement hit. I was too caught up in the other problems to even notice I was being scammed. When Jake took over for me, he...he saw the mess I'd made of everything. But it was too late even for him to help."

In a daze, Brianna sank down into her chair. *Evan* had been the one who ruined the company? *Evan* had been the target of Cy's scorn?

Evan expelled a harsh breath. "Maybe I *was* trying to compete with Jake. He's always been so damn good at everything. He went out on his own, played to his heart's content and still made a fortune. Don't look so surprised, Jake. Of course I kept up with what you were doing."

Jake muttered some wry retort while Cy launched into a sermon about risk, cash reserve and false growth.

Brianna, meanwhile, turned a stunned gaze on the man she'd been trying to groom into a credible CEO. All those times she'd berated him for his approach to business, pointed out how his brother would have done things.... He easily could have proven how ineffective Evan had been. Jake had known from the start that there were problems beyond the embezzlement, but he'd withheld all information that could point the finger of blame where it belonged. She thought of how he'd faced down the hostile crowd today, and how he'd taken her own accusations in stoic silence. He'd deliberately shouldered all responsibility.

With one glance at a wan, defeated Evan, she knew why Jake had done it. He'd been protecting his brother at a very vulnerable time in his life.

And she'd thought he didn't know how to love!

"So, Jake," Cy rumbled, his gaze now centered on the black sheep, "what do you suggest we do now?"

It was then, as every member of the board leaned forward attentively, that Brianna realized the full weight of their trust in Jake's expertise. They were turning to him for answers. In a very literal sense, the future of the company, of the town, of everyone she loved depended on Jake Rowland.

For the first time since the bad news had hit, a spark of hope kindled inside her.

"I wish I could offer you better options." His voice sounded gruff and weary. "You won't like any of them."

Brianna tightened her clasped hands. *Please say there's a way to save the company. Please!*

"If you try to keep the company running and invest more money in it, you'll only be throwing good money after bad. Once you've unloaded the large, costly accounts, it'll take too long to build up a solid book of smaller ones. Your best chance of getting anything out of your investment is to turn your accounts over to other insurance companies and liquidate the company's assets before too many claims hit."

Cy released a long breath. "I reached the same conclusion." The others grimly concurred. Jake fielded questions from all sides, answering one after another.

Brianna sat in heartsick silence. They were really going to do it—close down Rowland Insurance. All of their questions had to do with loss and profit. No one raised any objection to throwing in the towel. They'd already decided, she realized. They'd only been waiting for Jake to confirm what they already knew.

Any minute now, they'd turn to her with instructions on how to "disassemble" the workforce. And she'd have to go back to the office and carry out those instructions.

"Jake." The name had left her lips before she'd even meant to say it. "Jake!"

He halted in the middle of a discussion with the board and turned a questioning gaze to her. Murmurs continued around them like the humming of bees. "Don't do it, Jake. Don't close down the company."

"Brianna, the bottom line—"

"This is about more than just profit. It's about the town. Don't you know how special it is?" Her voice was wrought with emotion, and the others immediately fell silent. "When my mother brought me here as a child we didn't have a penny to our names, not even enough to stay on the bus and just pass through. We were homeless, Jake. Homeless!" She saw the flicker of surprise in his eyes and realized he hadn't known.

"The minister took us in," she said. "The community took us in, too, and helped my mother get back on her feet. I'll never stop loving them for that." She glanced around at the others. "Don't you want your grandchildren to live in a place where people care about each other? If you do, then you've got to care about *them.*" She gazed again at Jake, though she barely saw him through the sheen of tears that had somehow warped her vision. "This is my home. I made it my home...and it's yours, too, Jake. Save the company. If you care enough, *you'll do it!*"

Her throat had closed entirely, and Jake was little more than a motionless blur. Through silence thicker than any fog, she bowed her head and hurried from the room.

THE REC ROOM looked as it had when they'd been kids—pool table, pinball machine, trampoline, TV. Jake hadn't come here to reminisce, though; he'd come here to be alone while the others had lunch.

Absently he took a pool cue down from the wall and chalked its tip, pondering why Brianna had jumped to his defense. At first, he'd assumed she knew Cy had been referring to Evan. Her reaction would have made perfect sense. But then she'd said, "Terminate me without references, but I won't listen to you blame the company's downfall on *Jake!*"

He'd been astounded. She'd been defending him. All her magnificent fire and compassion had been on his behalf, and yet, just a week ago, she had accused him of playing reckless games and ordered him to stay away from her. After all that, she'd endangered the references she'd need to find another job by going up against the old man, chairman of the board, while he was in one of his rages, no less, in Jake's defense.

Mindlessly Jake racked up the balls on the green felt. Hope beat painfully like iron fists in his heart. She'd obviously changed her mind about him, but *how much?* Compressing his lips, he fought against the hope. He'd bled enough this past week, wanting her—wanting what he couldn't have.

He positioned his cue stick in careful aim and thought

of her plea: *Save the company, Jake. If you care enough, you'll do it.* For as long as he could remember, he'd fantasized about the moment Brianna Devon would turn to him with worshiping eyes and acknowledge what a terrific guy he really was. Lately it had become an obsession, wanting her to believe in him more than she believed in anyone.

He slid the stick through his fingers and hit the cue ball, scattering the multicolored balls. Why in the hell had she suddenly chosen now to show a little faith? Now, when the company was in shambles and the smartest course was to liquidate. Now, when all he wanted to do was advise the board and get the hell out of town before he had to watch her turn that tender gaze on Evan again.

He ricocheted one ball off another, which slid into the corner pocket. The woman was making him crazy. She wanted him to do something that would require a foolhardy risk. He'd have to merge his own lucrative little investment firm with the ailing insurance company and find other investors to back it. He'd have to lay everything he'd ever worked for on the line: his money, his business, his contacts. And if he failed, the failure would break him financially and professionally.

He'd lose the freedom that had always been so vital to his happiness. The days of hopping on a plane and going off to wherever he pleased would be over.

Why the hell would he even consider it? Because Brianna wanted to save her home? Because she'd called it *his* home, too? What would that mean when he was stuck here overseeing the new corporation and she was back in Evan's arms, deluding herself? Good Lord, she could end up being his *sister-in-law!* Jake's grip on the cue stick grew painful and cold, sick waves coursed through him.

He shouldn't be thinking about Brianna at all. He couldn't base a business decision of this magnitude on his feelings for a woman. But it meant so damned much to her—this company, this town. And whether he liked it or not, she meant everything to him.

"Mister Jake," Lucy called from the doorway, "I knew I'd find you down here playing. Cy's wantin' you."

BRIANNA HAD WALKED straight home from the meeting, too upset to talk to anyone from the office. She now sat on her sofa in painful contemplation of how she'd believed the worst about Jake, just as she always had. She'd accused him of playing reckless games with the company, and with her. She'd been wrong about the company. Maybe she'd been wrong about other things, too.

As she remembered the sweet love they'd made, pain cut through her, deep and sharp. As far as Jake knew, she'd used him for sex, then shoved him out of her life. Any chance they'd had of something more had died there and then.

And today, she'd had the gall to ask him to save her home. Why should he? Why should he give a damn?

A knock at her door jarred her. She peeked through the peephole and her heart expanded. *Jake!* Her face grew warm and her hands shook as she unlocked the door. But when she'd swung it open, she realized it wasn't Jake but Evan.

"Brianna, are you okay?" He patted her shoulder and squeezed it, studying her in concern.

"I'm fine." She swallowed her disappointment and

led him to the living-room sofa. "How are you holding up?"

"Better." Although he still looked grim, he seemed more in control of himself. "I'm glad everything's out in the open. And I'm sorry for the mess I've caused. I thought you'd want to know the outcome of the meeting."

"Outcome?"

"The board thinks Jake has lost his mind. He came back after lunch with the idea of merging his investment company with Rowland Insurance. Don't get your hopes up," he warned, but her hopes rose anyway. "Even Jake admits it's a long shot. He could end up broke. Neither Cy nor the board wants to get involved. He'll have to find backers with deep pockets. He's on the phone right now."

"He's risking his own fortune to save the company?" A volatile mix of hope and worry churned within her. "Why?"

"I thought you'd understand that better than I would." With a tilt of his head, he studied her. "There's something that's been right under my nose for years and I've never seen it. I knew how Jake always pestered you, but I thought it was just a game—a challenge, since you were the only girl he couldn't get."

Embarrassment stole over her to hear Evan discuss the matter, but he seemed lost in his own musings. "He had more fun hassling you than dating anyone else. In his wildest years, whenever he'd had one too many beers, he always brought up your name. When he got older, he was touchy whenever you were mentioned. And one time, during a ski trip, I overheard an argument coming from his bedroom in the chalet. His date had slapped him. From what she shouted, I gathered they'd been...uh...in bed...and he'd called her Brianna."

Her breath stopped somewhere between her heart and throat. Dare she believe what he seemed to be telling her?

"Jake loves a challenge, but he'd never let one interfere with his sex life," Evan reflected. "I should have paid more attention to all that." He lifted a shoulder in a shrug. "I didn't see it for what it was until this morning, outside Cy's door. The way Jake looked at you—and you at him—I'd have to be blind not to see that you're in love."

"Me?" she whispered.

"And Jake. Especially Jake. It didn't take twin telepathy for me to figure that out. I've spent ten years watching him make a fool of himself over you."

"Oh, Evan." Her voice caught. "I've been horrible to him. I wouldn't blame him if he never spoke to me again."

He handed her a key. "To my apartment," he said. "I won't be home tonight. There's someone I promised to meet, but Jake will have to stop by to pack before he heads out for the airport."

"Tonight? He's leaving tonight?"

Evan smiled and for a second looked identical to a mischievous Jake. "Not if you stop him first."

13

DARKNESS HAD FALLEN before Jake finished his phone calls at his grandfather's house, leaving him little time before his scheduled flight. Since Evan had left earlier with the car, Jake walked the few blocks home. The heaviness that had been riding in his gut worsened as he thought of his brother's destination.

"I'm going by Brianna's to settle some things," Evan had told him. Leaning closer, he'd whispered, "I never went to bed with her, you know. She wouldn't have me."

Jake clenched his jaw as he neared his apartment. He was glad to know that she and Evan had never made love. As much as he'd told himself it was none of his business, the issue *had* lurked somewhere in the murky darkness of his heart. But what had Evan meant by going to her house to "settle some things?" Had he been talking about their unconsummated affair? Had she given him some reason to believe she'd make love to him now?

On an impulse, Jake veered away from the stairway that led to his apartment and strode to his Maserati in the garage. He barely had enough time left to pack before his flight, but he couldn't leave town without knowing how things stood between Evan and Brianna.

Realizing how fast he was driving, he eased off the gas and loosened his fingers from their stranglehold on the wheel. A terrible irony mocked him: what if he'd erased the inhibition that had stopped her from making love to Evan?

No. He wouldn't allow himself to believe it. She hadn't been using him to further any sexual agenda, even if she'd claimed as much. She'd had nothing on her mind but him during their loving. He'd stake his life on it.

But that didn't mean she wouldn't take Evan back. Both had the crazy idea that platonic companionship could take the place of passion. Evan would torture himself with guilt by finding sexual release elsewhere, and Brianna would carry on as if nothing was wrong and spend her life in misery. He couldn't let that happen to either of them.

As he pulled up in front of her bungalow, he saw no car parked outside. Evan, for some reason, wasn't here. The house was dark; only the porch light was on. Apparently no one was home—unless she'd already gone to bed. He marched up to her door and rang the bell. "Brianna! Brianna?"

No one answered.

Acute emptiness gnawed at him. She had to be with Evan somewhere. He trudged back to his car. No sense in returning to the apartment; he didn't have enough time left to pack. Evan could send his things to his apartment in New York, where he would be coordinating the merger.

He sped off for the Columbus airport.

But as he reached the main highway, he pulled over onto the shoulder. He didn't want to leave this way. He didn't want to agonize all through the night, wondering if Evan and Brianna had mended their rift. And he was tired of rehashing every word she'd said in her passionate defense of him today, wondering if anything deeper than compassion lay behind it.

He'd be a fool to leave without knowing these things for sure. He drove home and parked his car in the garage. Evan's Mercedes sedan still wasn't there. Had he taken Brianna out for dinner somewhere? Resisting the urge to track them down, he climbed the stairs to the town house.

The windows, he noticed, were lit with a flickering glow, as if flames danced in the hearth. Evan wouldn't have left a fire burning unattended. Puzzled, he unlocked the door and walked in. Appetizing aromas wafted to him—grilled steak or chicken, maybe. The table, he saw, had been elegantly set for two, complete with candles and wineglasses.

"I wondered when you'd get home." The soft, low feminine purr drew his gaze to the shadows beside the fire.

His heart ceased to beat. She stood there...Brianna...in the sexy black cashmere dress she'd worn that very first night, her shapely shoulders bare, her hair a tawny, shimmering cloud. She looked good enough to die for. He felt as if he might.

She walked toward him, her gaze a warm invitation. Uncertainty threaded through her whisper, though, as she drew closer. "I...I wanted to surprise you."

Oh, she'd surprised him, all right. But she'd surprised him this way before. He wouldn't touch her, wouldn't pull her to him, even if the resistance killed him. In a voice too gruff and strained, he forced out, "I'm not Evan."

She stopped only inches away, so close that her familiar scent and warmth tantalized him with vivid, sensual memories. Her eyes widened and her surprise made every muscle in his body clench to ward off the fatal blow. *If she'd been waiting for his brother...*

"Do you really think I'd go back to Evan after what you and I had?" Hurt clouded the sensuality in her gaze. "Do you think I'd ever want him the way I want you?"

Strong, blessed relief washed through Jake, and his heart kicked into action, its rhythm hard and erratic. "No," he whispered. An awesome happiness loomed incredibly within his reach. He settled his hands around her narrow waist and savored the keen pleasure of touching her. "But there are some things about you that confuse the hell out of me."

She peered at him with the most beautiful eyes he'd ever seen—golden-green fire burning with both tenderness and desire. "Like what?"

"Like why I can't stop loving you."

Her lips parted in a silent cry, and her eyes glazed with emotion. *Meaning what?* His world paused for a heart-lurching moment. Then she slid her arms around his neck and brushed his mouth with a sensuous whisper, "I think we should delve further into that issue."

He did, with a kiss that thoroughly explored each facet of the question. She was heaven in his arms, exhilarating perfection, and he knew he'd never willingly live without her. But as the kiss ended, he wanted more reassurance than she'd given. "This isn't about erasing inhibitions, is it?"

"It never was," she confessed. "I was fooling myself. I was afraid of...of falling in love with you. But I did anyway."

He wanted so much to believe, he could barely speak. "You're not afraid now?"

"No." With clear and simple faith, she answered, "I

believe in you. And in me. I'm sorry it took so long for me to realize it."

He swallowed hard against the emotion expanding within him. "I might end up penniless. Broke."

"I know. Evan told me." She pressed closer against him, her love a shining beacon.

He didn't want to ruin the moment—the sweet, sharp, sanctifying moment—but he had to shine the light in even the darkest corners. "We might end up...homeless."

"No such thing, as long as we're together."

His love for her unfurled with a majesty that awed him. He met her in a powerful kiss. He lifted her in a fierce attempt to hold her closer and she wrapped her legs snugly around his hips, but even that didn't bring her close enough.

He wanted to be inside her.

As he carried her to the bedroom, he murmured against her ear, "I'm working this time on creating a new inhibition."

"A new one?" She drew back enough to search his face.

His stare smoldered into hers. "One that'll stop you from wanting to make love to anyone but me. Ever."

Her heart, already full, swelled with joyous love and secretive laughter. His gaze narrowed on her smile. She whispered, "That's been my hang-up all along."

He stopped in the bedroom doorway, stunned. A profound gladness soon glimmered in his dark blue eyes, but his brows converged. "We haven't erased it, have we?"

"Oh, no." She traced his bottom lip lightly with her tongue, then said in a throaty murmur, "It's only gotten worse."

He caught her in a deep, binding kiss—one that turned them around, tipped them against a wall, then tumbled them onto his bed. "I love you," he swore. "I love you."

She swore the same to him in every way she could. And though she'd always vowed to belong to no man, she did indeed belong to Jake—body, heart and soul.

She wanted it no other way.

Epilogue

IT HAD BEEN A summer of mergers, and looking back on it, the town of Pleasantville gathered around bonfires on the riverbank and lifted glasses of sparkling cider to the new corporation's five-year anniversary.

Cy Rowland himself had proposed the toast, proclaiming his grandsons to be "gutsy geniuses." Midwestern Insurance & Investment Corporation, under the direction of Jake, the day-to-day management of Evan, the nurturing of Brianna and the backing of employees and tycoons alike, had taken its place in the global economy as a thriving force.

Investors from around the country had joined them for the celebration—with good cause. The corporation had gone public, and the shares they'd purchased five years earlier had skyrocketed in value.

Many had become millionaires. One was Cort Dimitri, Jake's long-lost childhood pal, a quiet man of Greek ancestry who rarely smiled but toasted in pleased acknowledgment of his gain. His vivacious sister and soft-spoken mother mingled with neighbors they'd remembered with affection. Both ladies had cried joyous tears when Jake had first surprised them with a visit.

Another investor—Tyce Walker, the strikingly attractive detective who had captured the embezzler and invested his considerable fee—now stood surrounded by town folk who listened to how he'd tracked her down and recovered the stolen money. Most of the detective's audience was composed of women vying for his attention. Chloe settled the matter by putting a proprietary hand on his muscle-corded arm and taking him off for a grand tour of Pleasantville.

Watching the festivities from a blanket on the hillside, Brianna and Jake lounged in each other's arms as their three-year-old daughter picked dandelions. They celebrated the success of the *other* merger that had taken place that summer five years ago—the elaborate wedding of Brianna Devon and Jake Rowland.

That move had been risk free...and had surprised no one.

Take 4 bestselling love stories FREE

Plus get a FREE surprise gift!

Special Limited-time Offer

Mail to Harlequin Reader Service®

3010 Walden Avenue
P.O. Box 1867
Buffalo, N.Y. 14240-1867

YES! Please send me 4 free Harlequin Temptation® novels and my free surprise gift. Then send me 4 brand-new novels every month, which I will receive before they appear in bookstores. Bill me at the low price of $2.90 each plus 25¢ delivery and applicable sales tax, if any.* That's the complete price and a savings of over 10% off the cover prices—quite a bargain! I understand that accepting the books and gift places me under no obligation ever to buy any books. I can always return a shipment and cancel at any time. Even if I never buy another book from Harlequin, the 4 free books and the surprise gift are mine to keep forever.

142 BPA A3UP

Name _____ (PLEASE PRINT) _____

Address _____ Apt. No. _____

City _____ State _____ Zip _____

This offer is limited to one order per household and not valid to present Harlequin Temptation® subscribers. *Terms and prices are subject to change without notice. Sales tax applicable in N.Y.

UTEMP-696   ©1990 Harlequin Enterprises Limited

DELTA JUSTICE

**A family dynasty of law and order
is shattered by a mysterious crime
of passion.**

Don't miss the second Delta Justice book
as the mystery unfolds in:

Letters, Lies and Alibis
by Sandy Steen

Rancher Travis Hardin is determined to right a
sixty-year wrong and wreak vengeance on the Delacroix.
But he hadn't intended to fall in love doing it. Was his
desire for Shelby greater than his need to destroy her
family?

Lawyer Shelby Delacroix never does anything halfway.
She is passionate about life, her work...and Travis. Lost
in a romantic haze, Shelby encourages him to join her in
unearthing the Delacroix family secrets. Little does she
suspect that Travis is keeping a few secrets of his own....

**Available in October
wherever Harlequin books are sold.**

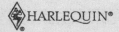

HARLEQUIN® *Temptation*

Their worlds collided in a torrid night to remember

Kat Kiley was a woman who knew passion but not love. J. P. Harrington was a man who knew love but not passion. They were as different as night and day, except that they both put their lives on the line for their work. Desperate circumstances brought them together, and from that moment on they were joined by destiny—whether they liked it or not.

Enjoy #660 *Heart and Soul* by Susan Worth.
Available in November 1997.

Sensuous stories from Temptation about heroes and heroines who share a single sizzling night of love....
And damn the consequences!

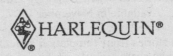